Christmas 2015

Dear Friends,

My favorite Christmas stories have always been romantic comedies, and the book you're holding in your hands is one of my favorite stories. As an author I know that if I laugh when writing a scene you'll laugh, too, and I laughed a lot. I believe Ashley and Dash are two of my favorite characters. And naturally there's a puppy involved.

The holiday season is often hectic, as we shuffle about among shopping, parties, family festivities, and everything else we can manage to squeeze in within a few short weeks. If ever there was a time a body needs to sit down, relax, and unwind, it's over the holidays. *Dashing Through the Snow* is my contribution to a peaceful, soothing evening.

One of my most frequently asked questions is: Where do you get your story ideas? This time I credit my husband. Wayne hates to fly and once jokingly said he wished someone would put him on a no-fly list. That was all it took for my mind to start buzzing with the question: What if????

Hearing from my readers is one of my most favorite things about the writing life. You can reach me through my website at debbiemacomber.com or on Facebook or Twitter. If you'd rather write, my mailing address is P.O. Box 1458, Port Orchard, WA 98366.

Merry Christmas!

Debbie Macomber

Dashing Through the Snow

DEBBIE MACOMBER

Dashing Through the Snow

A Christmas Novel

BALLANTINE BOOKS

NEW YORK

Copyright © 2015 by Debbie Macomber
Excerpt from *Mr. Miracle* by Debbie Macomber
copyright © 2014 by Debbie Macomber
Knitting pattern copyright © 2015 by Sheila Joynes

Published in the United States by Ballantine Books,
an imprint of Random House, a division of
Penguin Random House LLC, New York.

BALLANTINE and the HOUSE colophon are registered
trademarks of Penguin Random House LLC.

A trade edition has been simultaneously published
in slightly different form by Ballantine Books,
an imprint of Random House, a division of
Penguin Random House LLC.

LIBRARY OF CONGRESS CATALOGING-IN-PUBLICATION DATA
Macomber, Debbie.
Dashing through the snow : a Christmas novel / Debbie Macomber.
pages ; cm
ISBN 978-1-101-88540-6 (hardcover : alk. paper)
ISBN 978-0-553-39170-1 (ebook)
1. Christmas stories. I. Title.
PS3563.A2364D37 2015
813'.54—dc23
2015025744

Printed in the United States of America on acid-free paper

randomhousebooks.com

2 4 6 8 9 7 5 3 1

2015 Special Costco Edition

Book design by Dana Leigh Blanchette
Title-page image: © iStockphoto.com

To Dan and Mary Wolgemuth,
who understand the Reason for the Season

Dashing Through the Snow

Chapter One

"What? Are you kidding?" Ashley Davison couldn't believe what she was hearing. The reservation clerk for Highland Airlines glanced up nervously. "I'm sorry, but I can't sell you a ticket to Seattle. If you'd kindly step aside and wait a few minutes—"

"Can't or won't?" Ashley cut in, growing more frustrated and worried by the minute. She drew in a deep breath in an effort to control her patience. The woman behind the desk, whose name tag identified her as Stephanie, was clearly having a bad day. Getting upset with her, Ashley realized, wasn't going to help the situation. She made a determined effort to lower her voice and remain cool-headed.

"I . . . I can't. I'm sorry . . ."

Ashley refused to take no for an answer. Surprising her mother by flying home for Christmas was too important. "I understand getting a ticket to Seattle four days before Christmas is pushing my luck," she said, doing her best to appear calm and composed. "If I'd been able to book a seat sooner, I would have. Getting Christmas off from work was a complete surprise. I attend graduate school and I also work at a diner. I hated to miss the holidays with my mother, but I didn't have any choice. She's a widow and my brother lives in Texas and can't get home for Christmas, so there's only me." Perhaps if the reservation clerk knew her story, she might reconsider the *can't sell you a ticket* part of this discussion.

"Then my boss decided to close the diner between Christmas and New Year's for renovations after the refrigeration unit broke, and then he thought he may as well get a new deep fryer, too, so it just made sense to close down. All this happened at the very last minute, and because he felt so bad he gave me a Christmas bonus so I could fly home."

"I'm so sorry . . ." Stephanie said again, looking nervous. "If you'd kindly move aside and wait a few minutes."

"I haven't seen my mother since last August," Ashley continued, refusing to give up easily. "I wanted to surprise her. It would mean the world to both of us to be together over the holidays. Would you please look again? I'll take any seat, any time of the day or night."

Stephanie didn't so much as glance down at her computer screen with even a pretense of trying to accommodate her. "I can't . . . I wish I could, but I can't."

Ashley couldn't help but wonder what was up with this *can't* business. That made it all the more nonsensical.

"You *can't*," she repeated. "There must be more of an explanation than that. It just doesn't make sense."

The reservation clerk frowned. Her eyes roamed about the area as if she was looking for someone. That, too, was irritating. It was as if she was seeking a replacement or someone to rescue her.

"I believe you have your answer," the man behind her in line said impatiently. He shifted from one foot to the other, letting Ashley know he didn't appreciate her arguing with the clerk.

Ashley whirled around and confronted him face-to-face. "In case anyone forgot to mention it, this is Christmas. How about a little peace on earth and goodwill toward men? Be patient. I'll be finished as soon as possible and then you can talk to Stephanie, but for now it's my turn."

In response, he rolled his eyes.

Ashley returned her attention to the woman at the counter. "If you *can't* find me a seat on a plane to Seattle, I'd be willing to fly standby."

Stephanie shook her head.

"All the flights to Seattle are already booked?" The man next in line blurted out the question.

Stephanie's eyes widened as if she, too, was surprised he'd jumped into their conversation. "I . . . didn't say that. I'll speak to you directly in just a moment," she said.

"Excuse me?" Ashley flared, forgetting her resolve to remain calm and collected. This was too much. With her hands on her hips, she stared down at the other woman. "This is discrimination. Just because he's a man and good-looking you can dredge up a seat for him, but not for me?" This was gender discrimination. Where was a television crew when you needed one? This would make a juicy piece for the six-o'clock news.

Seeing that the line was getting long and the Grinch behind her wasn't the only one with a short fuse, Ashley decided to drop the entire matter.

"Okay, fine, have it your way, but I think this is just plain wrong." With that, she grabbed hold of her suitcase and with all the dignity she could muster started to walk away, feeling more stressed with each step.

"Miss, miss," the airline employee called after her. "If you'd kindly wait a few minutes I'm sure we could resolve this."

"No way," Ashley refused. "As you've repeatedly said,

you *can't* sell me a ticket." With that, she headed out of the airport with her dignity in shreds.

Ashley hadn't expected it would be easy to catch a last-minute flight. She'd already tried to find an available seat online, without luck. For reasons she couldn't understand she kept getting booted off the website. That was the reason she'd decided to come directly to the airport and try her chances there.

Naturally, flying home was her first option. But other modes of transportation were also possibilities. She could always try the bus or travel by train, if there was even one scheduled. The most expedient way to make the trip would be to drive. Unfortunately, her fifteen-year-old hand-me-down car wasn't in the best of shape and she was afraid of it breaking down along the way. To top it off, snow was predicted. Under normal circumstances, snow close to Christmas would be ideal, but not in an aging vehicle. If she could afford . . .

Ashley stopped mid-step. Why hadn't she thought of this earlier? She could always rent a car! The solution was right in front of her, the answer obvious. She should have thought about it long before now. And really there was no better place to rent a car than in an airport.

Perfect.

Reversing direction, Ashley headed toward the car rental

agencies, traveling down the escalator, rolling her suitcase behind her. When she reached the rental area, all of the agencies displayed signs that stated all their cars had been rented. All but one. Ashley made her way to that counter.

The longer she waited in line, the more she fumed about the airline clerk who'd insisted she *couldn't* sell her a seat. The nerve. And then to basically reassure the man in line behind her that there were seats available. That was discrimination of the worst kind, even if the guy was eye candy. Stephanie was clearly looking to do him a favor, which only served to irritate Ashley further. Truth be told, she'd noticed him, too. Hard not to, really. He was tall and stood with military precision, his dark appearance lean and strong. She suspected he was either military or former military. He gave that impression.

The line for the car rental agency slowly crept forward. As luck would have it, the very man who'd been so annoying at the airline counter came to stand behind her again.

It gave Ashley satisfaction to see he hadn't been any more successful with Stephanie in obtaining a seat than she had.

"So Stephanie couldn't sell you a seat, either," she said, trying hard not to gloat.

"All she had available was standby," he grumbled, fingering his cell.

Ashley would have gladly accepted a chance for a

standby flight. It wouldn't have mattered how long she had to wait. "Not good enough for you, I suppose."

He glanced her way and frowned, his look darkening. "I can't take the chance. I need to be in Seattle."

"I do, too," she insisted. "It's almost Christmas."

"This is for a job interview."

"A job?" Ashley echoed. "And you have to be there right before Christmas?"

Instead of answering, he returned his attention to his phone, frowning once again. Apparently he wasn't interested in making conversation with her. Fine. Whatever. That being the case, she wasn't interested in talking to him, either.

Turning back around, Ashley noticed that the line had progressed forward and that it was her turn next.

When the agent became available, she reached the counter and offered the man a warm smile, hoping not to have the same experience as she had with the clerk from the airline. "Merry Christmas."

The man looked harried and tired. Ashley didn't blame him. It was a hectic time of year.

"Merry Christmas," he returned without a lot of enthusiasm.

"I need to rent a car," she said, stating the obvious. "I'm headed to Seattle."

The agent looked down at his computer screen. "This is

your lucky day. You have the last car in the entire lot and my guess is it's the last vehicle in the entire airport."

"I'll take it," she said, beaming him a smile.

"Excuse me," the man behind her said. "Did I just hear you say that this is the last car you have available?"

It was all Ashley could do not to revel in her good luck and his lack of fortune. "And it's all mine." She couldn't resist rubbing it in. She was about to suggest he use his power-schmoozing techniques on the ticket agent upstairs again, but didn't. This car was hers. There was no need to taunt him any more than she already had.

"I'm sorry, sir, but I'm afraid it's all we have."

Ashley narrowed her eyes and glared at the handsome stranger.

"Okay, fine," he said, none too pleased. "Then I say we share it. That makes perfect sense, seeing that we both want to get to Seattle."

"It's not happening." Did Mr. *GQ* think she was stupid? Others might be influenced by his good looks and his charm, but not her. "For all I know, you could be a serial killer."

"Don't be ridiculous," he countered. "It's the perfect solution. I need to get to Seattle and so do you."

"I am not sharing this car with you!" Better safe than sorry.

"Miss," the agent interrupted. "If you're going to rent the car I'll need your credit card and driver's license."

"I fully intend to rent this car," Ashley said, glancing at the arrogant man standing next to her. She slapped her driver's license and credit card on the countertop and whirled around to face him.

"You're unbelievable," she told him, letting him know she wouldn't be pushed around. Some people might be taken in by this alpha male, but not her. It took more than a pretty face to win her over. "I'd be crazy to consider traveling with a complete stranger."

"Come on," he pleaded. "I'll pay for the car, accept all the responsibility, and you can ride for free."

"Oh sure. That's what you say now."

"It's a workable solution," the agent suggested. "It's a long drive to Seattle, and you'd both get what you want."

Ashley hesitated. It would be nice to save the money. And it was a good distance. Still . . .

"You'll pay all the expenses?" she asked the other man, eyeing him again, gauging his serial-killer potential.

"Gladly."

"Rental fee, insurance, gas? *Everything?*" If she agreed, she'd use her Christmas bonus for spending money.

"I'll pay for *everything*," he reiterated.

Still, she wasn't sure she should trust him. "How do I

know I can trust you?" she asked, eyes narrowing as she studied him. Sure, he looked decent enough, clean cut and all, but she'd seen enough true-crime shows on television to realize the killer was often the charming, handsome man no one suspected.

"You want references?" He made it sound like a big joke.

"Yes."

"Okay, fine." He exhaled as if completely put out, as if she was the one being unreasonable. "Who do you want to talk to? Will my mother do? What about my sister?"

"What about your wife?" If there was dirt to be had, the wife would be in the know. Besides, it made sense to alert the unsuspecting wife that he was about to travel with her.

"I'm not married."

"Okay, your girlfriend."

"I'm not involved at the moment." Just the way he spoke told her his patience was wearing thin. Too bad. She wasn't about to team up with someone she didn't know without a whole lot of assurances.

"Yeah, right." Men this good-looking never stayed out of relationships for long.

"Come on, lady, you have nothing to lose."

"I don't think so," she said.

"Miss Davison?" the agent said, returning her credit card and identification.

"Yes?"

"If I were you, I'd reconsider."

"You really should," Mr. Tall, Dark, and Handsome reiterated. "I'm taking on the responsibility and you'll ride for free. That's the deal. Take it or leave it."

Ashley hesitated and looked to the agent. "You really think I should do this?"

The agent nodded.

Ashley inhaled and did her best to size up the other man.

"Dash Sutherland," he said, and extended his hand. "If you want to talk to my mother, then I'd be happy to call her. You'll find I'm no evil threat to you or anyone else. We both need to get to Seattle and this is a viable solution."

Ashley had to admit she was tempted; still, she wasn't sure. "We'll drive straight through?"

"Whatever you want."

She chewed on her lower lip, indecision gripping her.

"Having a companion will make the drive easier," he said, encouraging her.

Ashley sighed. What tempted her most was the idea that he was willing to pick up all the expenses. And despite everything, she found herself attracted to him, which she wasn't entirely happy about.

"What more can I say to convince you?" he asked, growing impatient.

"Miss." The rental car clerk focused his gaze on her. "Take his offer."

Ashley studied the agent, not understanding why he was siding with this stranger. "Why do you care?"

The clerk met her look head-on. "Because I can't rent a car to anyone under twenty-five."

"Ah . . ." Ashley swallowed hard.

A smile slowly took over Dash's features as understanding came. "And you're not twenty-five, are you?"

Chapter Two

"My birthday was this month," Ashley said quickly, failing to mention she was twenty-four instead of twenty-five.

"I'm sorry," the man behind the counter said.

Ashley whirled around to face Dash, hoping with everything in her that he was still willing to extend his offer. His look was nothing short of gleeful at this piece of news.

"My name is Ashley. Ashley Davison."

His smile was slow to come. "You're singing a different tune now, aren't you, Ashley Davison?"

"Ah . . . yes." She folded her hands as if praying. "Would you be willing to share the car with me? I'll be happy to pay my half of the expenses."

Arrogant man that he was, Dash raised his eyebrows as he studied her without giving any indication of what he was thinking. Men like him were hard to read. It demanded strength of character to meet his gaze while he gave her the once-over.

"Can you provide me with references?" he asked.

"I suppose. Would my employer do?"

He disregarded the suggestion. "How do I know you're not one of those women who robs men blind at the first opportunity?"

This was too much. "You're kidding, right?"

He continued his study, slowly eyeing her up and down. "Not entirely. Better men than I have been fooled by that look of charm and innocence."

Ashley was a hair's space from losing her temper, but hesitated. He found her charming? That definitely softened the slight. "If anyone has cause to worry, it should be me."

"In that case, I have the perfect solution," Dash said, as he pressed his driver's license and credit card on top of the counter for the clerk to take. "You can always find another way of getting to Seattle."

"I'm willing to take my chances," Ashley said, quickly realizing her mistake.

He crossed his arms and appeared to be enjoying this far too much. "I'm not so sure I am."

"Listen, you two," the clerk said. "It's been a hectic morning and my shift is nearly over. Would you make up your minds so I can get out of here? I have a home, too, and I'd like nothing better than to get there within the next twenty-four hours instead of listening to the two of you bicker."

"Well?" Ashley asked, her heart in her eyes. "It would mean the world to me and my mother to be together for Christmas."

"You're sure you can trust me?" Dash asked, not bothering to hide his sarcasm. "Like you said, I could be a serial killer."

"I . . . I would feel better if I talked to someone who knows you."

"Like who?"

Seeing that he claimed he wasn't married, she offered an earlier suggestion. "I'd trust your mother."

Dash shared a look with the rental clerk. "Unbelievable."

"If I was her I'd feel better if I talked to someone, too," the other man said, siding with her.

"Okay, fine. You can talk to my mother while I fill out the paperwork." He reached for his cell, pressed a single button, and handed it to her.

It rang only once. A woman answered before Ashley had a chance to speak. "Dash, this is a surprise."

"Hello, Mrs. Sutherland?"

"Who is this?" the woman said, clearly surprised. "And what are you doing with my son's phone?"

"Dash gave it to me while he fills out paperwork for a rental car. There's only one car left in the entire lot and we're both headed to Seattle and, well, I thought if I talked to his mother I'd feel better about sharing a ride with a perfect stranger."

"Trust me, my dear, my son is far from perfect."

Ashley smiled. She hadn't met this woman and already she liked her. "I sort of picked up on that earlier."

The woman laughed. "I take it you want reassurances?"

"Yes, please. I asked to speak to his wife, but he claims he isn't married."

"He's telling you the truth, much to my chagrin. In my humble opinion he should have been married long before now, but he rarely listens to his mother. A good-looking man like Dash should have been married years ago. What's the matter with young people these days? By age thirty Larry and I had had both our children. These days kids don't feel the need to make a commitment."

Ashley lowered her voice. Really, this wasn't any of her business, but she was curious. "He isn't involved with anyone?"

"Not that he's mentioned to me, but then my son mostly keeps these matters to himself. It's all part of his army training. He's out now, thank heavens. He's responsible for every gray hair in my head."

"Oh."

"You sound like a nice, thoughtful girl. How old are you?"

"I just turned twenty-four."

"Married?"

"No. I'm in graduate school."

"Studying?"

"Social work."

"Excellent, excellent," she continued. "Let me assure you that you have no worries traveling with Dash. He's as stable as they come. He's headed to Seattle for this job interview with one of those big army contractors. He never really talks about what he did in the military. From what he said, it sounds like he worked on the computer guidance systems in drones."

"Oh, he's into software, then?"

"Yes, smart as a whip. Unfortunately, he doesn't appear to do as well with relationships."

That was interesting. "Really?"

"Too busy. He's always working, and being in the intelligence field didn't help matters. This job interview is important, otherwise I'd make a fuss about him not coming home for Christmas. According to Dash, it's the opportunity of a lifetime." She lowered her voice to a whisper.

"From what Dash said, this project with the private contractor is hush-hush. Even Dash doesn't know all the details; all he could find out is that the company wants to interview him right away."

"Wow." She was quickly becoming a woman who spoke in one-syllable responses.

"Rest assured you have nothing to fear from Dash. He's probably the safest person you could choose to travel with, and if he isn't, you call me and I'll give him a good tongue-lashing."

Ashley smiled and noticed that Dash had finished with the paperwork and was studying her through narrowed eyes. "You'd better give me the phone," he said, holding out his hand.

"In a minute," Ashley said, enjoying teasing him. She turned her back on him and started walking away. "Tell me more," she said, making sure her voice was loud enough to carry.

"Hand it over," Dash insisted, thrusting out his hand.

"Oh all right." Admittedly, she wasn't very gracious as she returned his cell.

Dash grabbed it and instantly demanded, "Mom, what did you tell her?" This was followed shortly by a burst of "Mom!"

Ashley batted her eyelashes at him. She shouldn't be enjoying this as much as she was. She wasn't sure what his mother said, but whatever it was, the conversation was over in seconds.

Ashley dutifully followed Dash to the waiting area for the bus that would drive them to the rental car lot. Sure enough, there was only the one car in the entire vicinity.

They thanked the driver and walked toward the car.

"I hope you're reassured I'm not going to take advantage of you," Dash muttered, as he opened the trunk. "I want it understood that despite what my mother might have said, I'm not interested in a relationship."

"Well, I'm not, either." Ashley bristled, refusing to admit she was disappointed. The men she met at school and the diner were often not worth the effort.

"Fine, then we understand each other."

"Perfectly," she assured him, and felt inclined to add, "Besides, you're not my type." She didn't really have a type, and if she did, he'd be at the top of the list, not that she'd tell him that.

"Oh, really?" he said. He snorted a laugh as if to say the opposite sex found him irresistible.

"You might think all women will fall for that strong, mysterious persona, but not me. I've got to finish school before I even think about getting involved with anyone." That part was true.

"Do you mind if we talk about something else?" he said, looking bored.

"No problem."

He placed his suitcase in the car's trunk and reached for hers.

"I can lift my own, thank you very much."

He raised both hands and stepped back. "Fine with me, have it your way."

Lifting the large suitcase was harder than she realized. Ashley had stuffed the bag as full as she could with clothes and gifts and everything else she thought she might need for the next seven days.

She snuck a peek at Dash, who rolled his eyes, which she pretended to ignore.

When she'd finished loading her suitcase, he opened the driver's-side door. His phone beeped and he reached for it, apparently reading a text message. She couldn't afford another smartphone. Hers had gone through the washing machine. Now she had only an old flip-top style that she hoped would last her until Christmas. He removed his coat, opened the back door, and tossed his jacket inside before climbing into the driver's seat. Ashley got into the car, too.

Once comfortable, she snapped the seatbelt in place and casually asked, "What kind of name is Dash, anyway?" To her way of thinking, his mother must have needed to get to the hospital in a hurry. She once met someone named Rush. He got the name because he arrived early and his mother said he was in a rush to make his grand entrance into the world.

"I was named after Dashiell Hammett."

"Do you have a sister named Lillian?" she asked, half joking.

Dash regarded her with fresh eyes, as if surprised she'd made the connection. "As a matter of fact, I do."

"Dashiell Hammett and Lillian Hellman are both great authors." Ashley had read their work and long admired their stories, particularly Lillian Hellman's.

"They were lovers for many years," Dash added. "My parents were avid fans. Dad devoured Dashiell's work and Mom liked Lillian Hellman's, hence our names."

As Dash drove out of the parking lot they were met with a long string of police vehicles that raced toward the airport, red lights flashing. Ashley sat up and took notice. Whatever was happening was big.

"I wonder what that's all about." she said.

"Check your phone," he suggested.

Ashley snorted. "I wish I could. I don't have Internet on my phone. My smartphone died a terrible death, so for now I'm stuck with this flip phone."

"You're joking."

"Hey, it's a phone."

"Check the radio, then."

Ashley spent several minutes going from station to station, but they didn't find anything to update them on a situation at the airport.

"It's probably a practice drill of some sort," she suggested.

He didn't look convinced. "That's doubtful. Thankfully, we were able to avoid the delay."

"Good timing on our part," she said, pleased to have escaped the excitement.

After a bit, Ashley settled back and was actually starting to get comfortable. It was a relief to let someone else maneuver through the heavy San Francisco traffic, following the freeway signs that would lead them out of town.

"Your mom is great," she said, picking up the conversation.

"Because she named me Dash?"

"Not entirely . . . I mean, that's only part of the reason. Your mother's refreshingly open. She told me how important this job interview is to you and insisted that you're completely trustworthy."

"And you believed her?" he asked, arching his thick eyebrows suggestively.

"Shouldn't I have?" She sat up a bit straighter.

"You tell me."

"You're not scaring me, even if you're one of those secret agents."

"I was never a secret agent," he flared.

"Hey, don't take it personally. Your mother said you did something with the guidance systems with drones."

Dash's mouth thinned. "She shouldn't be telling you anything about my military career."

"Why not?"

"Because it's none of your business."

Well, well, she certainly got put in her place. "Might I remind you I wasn't the one who asked to share this car."

"That was my mistake," he freely admitted.

They sat in silence for a couple of minutes before she asked, "Is your sister married?"

He diverted his gaze from the road and glared at her. "Why do you want to know?"

"I'm just making conversation."

"Well, don't. My family is my business."

"Okay, then. Sorry."

Ashley crossed her arms and turned her head, looking out the side window. The silence felt strained and awkward. She'd rather they were trading insults than sitting in this uncomfortable silence. She reached for her large purse and held it open on her lap as she dug through it.

"What are you looking for?" he asked, as she started divesting her bag of several items. She set her money case to one side and then her makeup bag, followed by her nail file and fingernail clippers, apartment and car keys, and a small bag of tissues.

Dash's gaze followed her action. "What's in there that's so important?" he demanded.

"A protein bar."

"You're hungry?"

"No, but I think you must be." Thankfully, she had two.

He snorted as if he found her response nothing short of humorous. "Do you have a gauge that lets you know other people's hunger index?"

"You're cranky," she explained, "and that's a good indicator. You didn't have breakfast, did you?"

"No," he admitted grudgingly.

"It's almost time for lunch."

He grumbled a reply: "And I'm not stopping."

"Whatever," she muttered back. She found what she was looking for and held it up triumphantly as she peeled back the wrapper and handed it to him.

He ignored her. "I'm not eating that."

"Why not? It's perfectly good." She took a bite of her own to prove her point and rubbed her tummy as if it was the most delicious thing she'd ever tasted. "Don't tell me you're too proud to admit you're hungry."

"I. Am. Not. Cranky." Each word was pronounced distinctly.

"So you say. Consider it a peace offering, if that makes a difference."

Reluctantly he reached for the bar and bit off the first half in a single bite.

"You'll feel better," she said, wanting to reassure him, pleased that he'd followed her advice.

"You're one of those women who takes delight in saying 'I told you so,' aren't you?"

"Only when I'm right," she said, grinning.

He snorted and finished off the bar and handed her the empty wrapper.

She waited a couple of minutes. "Feeling better?"

"Yes. Are you going to rub it in?"

"I could, but I won't. It's a long drive and it'd help if we got along. Agreed?"

"Yeah, I guess."

That was a step in the right direction. They made good time and Ashley found herself dozing in the warm car, daydreaming—and she hated to admit this—about Dash. She wondered what it would be like if they kissed. When she stirred she was surprised to find that they'd been on the road nearly two hours.

"I could use a rest stop," she said, seeing a road sign stating there was one just ahead.

"Okay. Did you enjoy your nap?"

Ashley stretched her arms and yawned. "I did."

"Has anyone ever told you that you snore?"

"I most certainly do not." She was insulted that he would even suggest such a thing.

He chuckled. "Wanna bet?"

"Yes, I wanna bet. I wasn't even fully asleep. I'd know if I snore, and I don't. You're saying that to get a rise out of me."

She did her best to quell her indignation and glanced over to see that Dash was struggling to hold back a smile. Just as she suspected, he was teasing her and enjoying it. She smiled. "You're flirting with me."

"What? By telling you I heard you snore?"

"Sounded like a flirt to me."

He laughed as though he found her accusation ridiculous, but even as he denied it, he was smiling.

Dash exited the freeway and pulled into the rest area, angling the car into an empty parking slot.

Ashley opened the door and climbed out, stretching her arms above her head. A shiver ran down her spine. It was much colder outside than she'd expected.

Dash grabbed his coat and searched through his pockets, then tossed it back inside and bent over the front seat.

"What are you looking for?" she asked.

"My phone."

"Did you lose it?"

"It's here," he barked. "It's got to be. Did you take it?"

"Of course not." It irritated her that he'd even suggest such a thing. "I have my own phone, remember?"

"I can't find it," he complained.

"It has to be there," she insisted, and wanting to help, she opened the passenger door on her side, looking on the floor.

"See anything?" Dash asked.

Ashley shook her head. "No."

"What could have happened to it?" he asked.

Ashley shrugged. The last thing she remembered was seeing him slip it inside his coat pocket.

"You got a text, remember?"

He frowned, narrowing his eyes as though searching through his memory bank.

"I saw you place it inside your coat pocket," she reminded him.

"And then I tossed my coat in the backseat."

"It isn't in your pocket?"

He glared at her, and that was answer enough.

"It must have fallen out of the car."

"You think?"

"Well, it wasn't my fault."

Dash looked sick. His shoulders sagged and he wiped a hand across his face. "It's lost now."

Chapter Three

Highland Airlines employee Stephanie Arness nervously clenched her hands together in her lap as she studied the FBI man standing over her. They'd sequestered her in a room inside the airport in order to question her. Another agent remained behind her and out of view.

"Let's go through this one more time," Agent Jordan Wilkes insisted, waving his hand at her as he slowly paced the area in front of her chair.

"But I've already told you everything I know," Stephanie protested. Wilkes had been interviewing her for the last sixty minutes and there wasn't anything she hadn't told him a dozen times or more. Apparently, she'd failed to follow proper protocol and didn't contact the authorities soon enough when she'd found Ashley Davison's name on the no-fly list. This interrogation appeared to be the price she had to pay.

Agent Wilkes chose to ignore her plea. "Humor me. Let's start at the beginning one more time."

"Okay," Stephanie said, drawing in a deep breath and doing her best to remain calm and outwardly patient. "A young woman in her midtwenties approached the counter and asked to purchase a ticket to Seattle."

"Did she state a particular flight or time?" he asked— actually, it was more of a demand than a question.

Stephanie had already answered this same question repeatedly. "No, the woman said she was willing to take any seat day or night, it didn't matter."

He nodded, as if Stephanie should continue.

"When I entered her name, Ashley Davison, into the computer it immediately came up on the no-fly list and as an FBI person of interest, suspected of terrorist activity. I was instructed to immediately notify the FBI and airport security."

"Which you delayed doing, right?" The question was followed by an intense glare.

"I tried," Stephanie insisted, "but Ms. Davison kept arguing with me. I repeatedly asked her to step aside and wait. I hoped to get in touch with security, but she continued talking and insisting that I get her a flight. I couldn't hold a conversation with her and call for security at the same time. I'd hoped to keep her at the desk long enough for airport security to arrive, but then I realized that I hadn't put in the call and the man standing behind her got impatient and—"

Agent Wilkes stopped her. "What man? This is the first time you mentioned anyone else."

"He was just another passenger behind her who got impatient that Ms. Davison was taking up so much time when there was a long line of customers waiting."

"He wasn't with her?"

"No." She hesitated. She hadn't considered this. "At least I don't think so."

"You're sure about that?"

Stephanie closed her eyes and mentally reviewed the scene as it played out in her mind. After thinking it over she was fairly certain they weren't connected. She gradually shook her head.

"I doubt it, but . . ." She wasn't sure this was significant, and so stopped talking.

"But what?" Agent Wilkes insisted. "This could be important."

"The man was also hoping to get on a flight to Seattle."

Agent Wilkes stopped pacing and looked across the room at a second agent, who had remained quiet for a good part of the interview. "Did you hear that, Buckley?"

Agent Buckley nodded and approached Stephanie. He reached for a pad and started to take notes.

"Do you happen to recall this man's name?" Agent Buckley asked.

He'd been good-looking, but she hadn't really paid attention to his name. Stephanie shook her head. "Sorry, no."

"Think again." Agent Wilkes insisted, none too gently.

Stephanie closed her eyes and did her best to bring up the memory of their short conversation. Unfortunately, she couldn't recall seeing anything with his name listed.

"I don't believe he ever said his name."

"Did he take out his identification? People do that instinctively when looking to book a ticket," he reminded her.

As hard as she tried, Stephanie couldn't remember seeing anything with his name. "I would have remembered if he had," she insisted.

"Oh, and why's that?"

She shifted in her seat and looked down in an effort to hide her embarrassment. "He was the kind of man women notice."

"How's that?"

"He was good-looking. Muscular . . . you know, physically fit, with one of those very short haircuts."

"You mean a military cut?"

"Yeah, like that, and really the most incredible dark eyes. Real dark."

"Sinister?"

"Oh, not at all. More like 'look all you want, but you can't have me' eyes."

The two agents glanced at each other and frowned.

"You writing that down, Buckley?"

Buckley snorted. "Not on your life."

"Did you sell this man a ticket?"

"No. He claimed he had to be in Seattle before December twenty-second and couldn't take a chance with standby. He needed a guaranteed seat and was willing to pay whatever it cost."

The two agents froze. "The twenty-second, you say?"

"Yes." She specifically recalled the date because it was the last day she was scheduled to work before taking time off for the holidays.

"Do you think we should put Seattle on alert?" Buckley asked.

Agent Wilkes shook his head. "It's too early. We need more information."

"Right."

Agent Wilkes returned his attention to Stephanie once again. "What did you tell him?"

"The only thing I could. The only tickets available this

close to Christmas were standby." She wasn't sure why the FBI agents were so curious about this man when she was convinced Ashley Davison and the looker weren't connected.

Then Stephanie remembered something else. "That was when the woman . . ."

"Ashley Davison," he supplied.

"Yes, Ms. Davison got terribly upset. She wanted to know why there was a possibility he could fly standby and she couldn't."

"And what did you tell her?"

"Nothing, but really you can't blame her for being put out. I think a couple of people waiting in line agreed with her. Ms. Davison said this was gender discrimination because I chose to give the man a seat and not her."

"Which is when you told her to kindly wait to the side?"

"Yes, but I'd been telling her that all along." Stephanie couldn't imagine why she had to repeat this story over and over again, but she was beginning to understand now. Each time she told it she remembered some other small detail, like the man behind Ashley Davison in line. "I wanted to call security to come for her, but she took off right away."

"And you didn't see which direction she went?"

Stephanie felt like a complete failure. She should have looked, but had gotten distracted by the man behind Davison in line, apologizing for keeping him waiting and explaining that she needed a minute while she reached for the phone. By the time she was able to connect with security, Ashley Davison was out of sight.

"You're sure you didn't see the direction in which she was headed?"

"No, sorry."

Agent Buckley must have noticed her distress, because he said, "You've been helpful."

"I wish I'd known to ask for more information."

The door opened and a female agent entered the room.

"What did you learn from the surveillance tape?" Agent Wilkes asked.

The woman, Agent Bass, remained expressionless. "The camera isn't focused on the Highland Airlines counter, so we weren't able to get a clear photo of the woman."

"What about after she left the counter?"

"We think we might have found her from the description provided by the reservation clerk."

The only known photo available of the bombing suspect was blurred, but it gave enough detail to possibly identify her, Wilkes had explained earlier. He'd shown what he had to Stephanie, but she'd been unable to make a positive identification.

"The airport was crowded and it took some time to pick her out."

"Is there a clear shot of her face?"

The female agent exhaled. "She's clever. Her head is lowered, so we were unable to get positive facial recognition."

"Figures," Agent Wilkes muttered.

Agent Bass agreed. "It's almost as if she knew where the camera was situated and when to look down."

"Anything else of significance?"

"The suitcase. She's dragging a large suitcase with her. It looks to be heavy."

The Highland Airlines clerk watched as the two male agents made eye contact. She wasn't sure why this fact would be significant, but from their reaction, clearly it was.

"Would you be able to pick out the man who was at the counter with Ms. Davison?" Agent Wilkes asked, directing the question at her.

Right away Stephanie nodded. The looker had a face she wouldn't soon forget. All that chiseled manhood would be hard to miss. Even now she got goose bumps just thinking about him. She really would have liked to help him, but there wasn't anything she could do. All the Seattle-bound flights were booked solid, and overbooked in some instances.

"Show her the surveillance tapes," Agent Wilkes instructed the female agent.

"Right away."

Wanting to leave the room where she'd been cooped up

for the better part of an hour, Stephanie was more than happy to stand up and move about.

"I'm Agent Bass," the other woman said, introducing herself as she led Stephanie out of the room. "Carlene Bass."

"Stephanie Arness," she said, following the other woman's lead.

"You've been a big help, Stephanie."

"Thank you." The other woman walked at a quick pace and Stephanie had to half trot in order to keep up with her. Although she'd worked for the airlines for five years, she'd never been in the area where the FBI agent took her now.

The compact room looked like the inside of a busy television station, with a long row of video screens showing a variety of activities taking place all at the same time in multiple areas of the airport.

"Can we show Ms. Arness the footage we discussed earlier?" Agent Bass asked the technician. Next she led Stephanie to a chair and indicated she should take a seat.

The technician typed in a few keystrokes and a video started to play on the screen in front of Stephanie. The scene looked like something out of a movie, with people hustling and bustling about. Mothers steered their children toward the security gates while others simply tried to move from one area to another.

Stephanie studied the faces as best she could and wasn't able to identify a single one. She'd thought it would be easy to point out the looker, but that proved to be far more difficult than she assumed it would be.

"That's the woman we believe to be Ashley Davison from the description you provided," Agent Bass said, pointing toward the screen, and the technician froze the frame.

Stephanie squinted and shook her head. "That could be her." From this angle it was nearly impossible to make out any facial identification. "That's the coat she wore and she's carrying the same purse," Stephanie conceded. The more she stared at the technician's screen, the more convinced she became.

"We've had Ashley Davison on our list for the last two years. This is a surprise. The most recent information we have indicated she was in Texas."

Stephanie hated to appear naïve, but she had an important question. "If she's so clever, then why is she using her real name?"

"Good question," Agent Bass said, nodding approvingly. "It's one I asked myself. If I wanted to get to Seattle in a hurry and knew that I was on a person-of-interest list for the FBI, then I would use an alias and fake ID."

"Right." That was totally reasonable. Why risk capture by using her real identity? It made no logical sense that Ashley Davison would make herself such an easy target. It was almost as if she was asking to be held up and questioned.

"Agent Wilkes thinks that she thrives on risk and what looks like a misstep is actually pure genius."

"In what way?" Stephanie held her breath, convinced she was about to get insider information she'd be able to pass along to her friends.

"This might actually be a ploy to send us off in the direction of Seattle when she's headed for L.A. But we have every intention of finding her before she has the opportunity to follow through with whatever her plans might be."

"She's . . . dangerous?" A chill went up Stephanie's spine. Looking at her, no one would believe it. Ashley Davison looked as normal as anyone else. She was short, with big brown eyes and long brown hair—as American as apple pie. Cute, too.

Agent Bass hesitated. "We believe Davison is tied in with a terrorist organization and is already responsible for one bombing."

That said, Agent Bass gestured for the technician to continue with the security tape.

As best she could, Stephanie studied the monitor, keeping her concentration focused on the video of the moving throng of people who flashed across the screen. It didn't take long for her to recognize the man who'd been at the counter.

"There," she cried, pointing at him. Actually, it was just as easy as she'd hoped it would be. He was several inches taller than those around him. He looked intent and was heading in the same direction as Ms. Davison. "That's him."

"You're sure?"

"Absolutely." She punctuated her comment with a nod.

Once more the technician froze the frame and Agent Bass connected with her two male counterparts. "We've ID'd him. Full-frontal view. I'm sending it on to Langley for facial recognition." She listened for a moment and then said, "Right away."

Stephanie could hear voices but was unable to make out what was being said.

Just before Stephanie stood to vacate the room, Agent Bass had her answer. She reached for her cell and connected with the other agents. "His name is Dashiell Sutherland, ex–army intelligence."

Stephanie saw the agent's reaction as she immediately tensed and disconnected the phone.

"What does that mean?" Stephanie asked.

It was almost as if the other woman had forgotten she was in the room. "We want to thank you again for all your help," Agent Bass said, letting Stephanie know that they were finished with her. "You're free to go now. If we need any further information we'll be in touch."

As eager as she'd been to get away, Stephanie was even more curious to find out what the FBI was thinking.

"I'm fairly certain the two had never seen each other until today," she said, coming to the man's defense, although she couldn't be one hundred percent positive. All the banter between them might have been for show.

"Agent Wilkes disagrees, but that's neither here nor there."

Agents Buckley and Wilkes joined their fellow agent in the room. "If you weren't able to get a flight to Seattle when you needed to be in the area for a certain amount of time, what would you do?" Agent Wilkes asked, as a rhetorical question.

"I'd rent a car," Stephanie suggested, although she was fairly certain they weren't interested in her opinion.

"That's what I'd do," Agent Bass concurred.

"We're already checking," Wilkes confirmed to his fellow agents.

Chapter Four

Dash was clearly upset that he'd lost his phone. His jaw was clenched and he glared at Ashley as if she were personally responsible. She was about to defend herself but assumed it'd be best to keep her mouth closed and smile sweetly . . . until he gave a disgusted grunt and shook his head. At that point she'd had enough.

Ashley held up both arms as if he'd pulled a gun on her. "Hey, it wasn't my fault. You were the one who tossed your coat in the backseat. Did you consider that it might have fallen out?" That was the only explanation that made sense.

"That phone was less than a month old," he muttered.

"It is what it is. Accept it." She was unwilling to sit in a car with him for however many miles while he stewed over a lost phone.

"Easy for you to say."

She agreed with him, but there was nothing they could do about it now. From the scowl he gave her she could tell her advice wasn't appreciated.

"I thought you said you needed a restroom."

"I do."

He looked toward the building. "Are you waiting for a handwritten invitation?"

"No . . . but listen, you can use my phone if you need to . . . I don't mind."

"Big of you."

"Hey, I'm only trying to be helpful."

Dash plowed his fingers through his hair. His shoulders sagged as he exhaled slowly. "You're right. Sorry."

She gave him credit for the apology. The truth was she'd been upset, too, when her smartphone ended up in the washer and dryer. It'd taken her a while to get over the frustration of her own stupidity, and now she figured Dash needed time to stew. He'd get over it soon enough, she hoped.

She reached for her purse and headed toward the restrooms. As she walked toward the building she noticed a man at a small outbuilding wearing a cap that stated he was a Vietnam veteran. He was apparently a volunteer for the

VFW offering free coffee and cookies to travelers. A large jar was set out for donations. She didn't know about Dash, but she could certainly do with a cup.

As soon as she finished in the facilities, she approached the coffee stand and the vet. "Merry Christmas," she said, beaming him a smile. She opened her purse and took out a few dollars and placed them inside the donation jar.

"Merry Christmas," the vet returned, and then to her surprise added, "I don't suppose I could interest you in a free puppy?"

"A puppy?" she repeated. "I came for coffee." She pocketed a couple of cookies as well.

"Sure, sure, help yourself to the coffee, but while you're here, think about the puppy."

Ashley didn't see any puppies. "What's the deal?"

Frowning, the vet shook his head. "I don't know what's the matter with people these days. I showed up this morning and found a whole litter of puppies someone had dumped in a box in the parking lot. Poor little buggers were near frozen to death. I brought them in here where it's warm and gave them some milk and now I'm looking to find them homes."

"Have you had any luck?"

"Gave three away already. I only have one left."

"Really."

"Cute as can be. Why don't you take a look?"

Ashley was tempted. Pickles, the family dog, had died six months ago, and her mother was an empty nester. Ashley knew her mom missed Pickles. Recently, her mom had mentioned she wanted another dog, but she hadn't finished grieving for the rescue dog she'd loved.

"Okay," Ashley said, already feeling her heart weaken.

"You'll take him?"

Quickly she shook her head. "I'll take a look . . . no promises."

"Good enough." The vet stood and opened a door on the side of the structure to let her inside. "He's over here," he said, pointing toward a large cardboard box tucked up close to the heater. A brown puppy of indistinguishable breed was cuddled up on a towel, sound asleep.

Ashley squatted down by the box and the puppy lifted his head and stared directly at her. He had dark round eyes that seemed to look straight through her. She petted his head, and then, as if he'd been trained to weaken her resolve, he licked her hand. He was simply adorable and her heart melted as he rose and stretched upward, bracing his front paws on the edge of the box. His melting brown eyes connected with hers as if to say "Take me, take me."

"Don't know what breed he is," the vet said. "Looks like a mixture."

Ashley agreed. "I'd say he'll probably grow to maturity at twenty or twenty-five pounds."

The Vietnam vet nodded. "That would be my guess. Not too big and not too small."

"How old do you think he is?"

The vet shrugged. "Your guess is as good as mine. Maybe six or eight weeks. What kind of person just abandons puppies like this?"

Ashley didn't have an answer for him. "Someone without a heart," she suggested.

"Guess whoever did was thinking people traveling this time of year would be willing to find homes for them. I'd adopt one myself, but the missus wouldn't take kindly to me bringing home a puppy when we just put in new carpet. The last one chewed up several of her expensive shoes—" He stopped abruptly. "I don't want that to dissuade you, though. Just make sure you give him a chew toy."

"I was thinking of my mom," Ashley said, biting down on her bottom lip. "Mom lost Pickles and really misses him. He was a great companion; I know she'd like another dog."

"Sure would make her a nice Christmas gift, then, don't you think?" the vet said, looking hopeful. "I hate to pressure you, but my shift is over in two hours and if I don't find him a home, I'll have to drop him at the shelter."

Ashley picked up the puppy and tucked him in her arms and kissed the top of his head. He immediately cuddled up against her. She knew animal shelters were often crowded and her heart squeezed. It was then that she knew what she had to do. She reluctantly returned the puppy to the box.

"So what do you think?" the war vet asked eagerly.

"I'll take him, but—"

"The minute I saw you," the vet said, interrupting her, "I said to myself, 'There's a woman with a heart. She'll take this puppy for sure,' and I was right."

Ashley wished it was that easy. "Before I can take him I need to check with my traveling companion." The rental car was in Dash's name. He was the one responsible for the car, not her, and he would need to agree.

"Sure, sure," the vet said. "No problem; take your time. I'm not going anywhere for the next two hours."

"I'll be right back." Ashley straightened and hurried to the car, taking two cups of coffee and several cookies with her.

Dash was sitting inside the vehicle, tapping his finger against the steering wheel, impatiently waiting for her. It didn't look like his mood had improved since he'd discovered he'd lost his phone. She approached the driver's side with a foam cup of steaming coffee. Dash rolled down the window.

"Do you take anything in your coffee?"

Frowning, he shook his head. "Nothing."

"You sure? A little sugar might help your disposition."

His frown darkened. "Very funny. I like my coffee black."

"Okay." She handed him the coffee and a handful of store-bought cookies the veterans' organization provided.

"Thanks," Dash said after taking the first sip.

Ashley remained standing by the driver's side.

"You ready to leave?"

"I have a question."

He paused and glanced at his watch, letting her know he didn't appreciate the delay. "What is it?"

"Did you have a dog when you were growing up?"

"Yes. So what? Come on, let's go."

"Just curious," she said, gifting him with a dazzling smile. "What kind of dog was it?"

"A Dachshund. Is there a point to this conversation?"

"Just curious." She bit into her bottom lip. "Someone abandoned a litter of puppies here in the parking lot this morning. The vet serving coffee found them."

His gaze softened. "That's tough."

"He's looking for homes and has found three people who were willing to help. I was thinking—"

"Ashley, no," he said, as if reading her thoughts. "As much as I'd like to help, we can't take a puppy with us. You forget that they poop and pee and are a hassle."

"He wouldn't be any trouble. I'd take care of him, and seeing that we're driving straight through, I thought—"

Again, he interrupted her. "I had the radio on while you were in the restroom and there's snow predicted. We might be forced to spend the night somewhere on the road, which puts me on an even tighter schedule. I can't miss this interview."

"We lost Pickles this last summer," she told him, refusing to give up so easily.

"You named your dog Pickles?"

She brightened. "Cute, isn't it?" She didn't mention that she'd been the one to choose his name.

He shook his head. "It's ridiculous. Poor dog probably died of embarrassment."

"That's not kind," she flared.

"Okay, fine, I apologize. We need to get back on the road. I'm sorry about the dog. Someone else will give him a good home."

"The man says he'll have to leave the puppy at a shelter if he doesn't find someone to take him. And besides, the puppy chose me."

"What?"

"Never mind, you wouldn't understand. Before you say no, come and take a look at him. That's all I'm asking."

"Not going to happen."

"Why not?" Now Dash was starting to irritate her.

"I already explained why. Now either you get in the car or I'm leaving you."

"You wouldn't do that."

"Don't tempt me. I'm already regretting agreeing to

travel with you and I'm not in the best of moods as it is. I suggest you get in the car now."

Her head came back. "You regret traveling with me?" And this after she'd shared her protein bars and brought him coffee.

He didn't answer.

"That comment was unnecessary."

"I'm not in the mood. I feel bad about the puppy, but he isn't your problem and he certainly isn't mine, so get in the car."

Her feelings were hurt, and she'd thought they were getting along so well, too. To this point she'd enjoyed spending time with him and found him easy company. Apparently, she was wrong. "I thought you were a better person than this."

"Well, I'm not. You can stop looking at me with those big sad eyes because it isn't going to do you any good. Are you coming or not?"

"But—"

"Come on," he said impatiently. "You're becoming a nuisance."

"I'm sorry about your phone, I really am, but I promise you a puppy won't be the least bit of trouble . . ." She paused and widened her eyes. "Wait. What do you mean I'm a nuisance?"

He glared back at her.

"Fine, then. Open the trunk," she insisted.

"What?"

"You heard me."

"We're in the middle of nowhere."

This was a bad idea. A really bad idea. She needed to think this through more carefully. She waited, hoping Dash would apologize or stop her.

He didn't.

"Take back what you said," she demanded.

Now he looked as if he was about to burst out laughing. "What is this? I haven't heard that since I was in grade school."

"You're mad about your phone and you're taking it out on me and that poor abandoned puppy." She stretched her arm out behind her, pointing to the coffee stand. "If you took one look at him you'd change your mind."

"The only thing I'm changing my mind about is you." He popped the lever that released the trunk latch.

"Are you going to apologize or not?"

"No."

"Will you at least look at the puppy?" she tried again. It was the least he could do. "I'll accept that over an apology."

"No," he stubbornly replied.

Her heart shot to her throat as she stared at the open trunk. Dash had thrown down the gauntlet and called her bluff. With her head held high and swallowing hard, Ashley walked around the vehicle and with some difficulty lifted her heavy suitcase out of the trunk and set it down on the asphalt. With exaggerated care she closed the trunk again, all the while praying Dash would back down.

Wheeling her suitcase behind her, she made her way across the parking lot and looked back at Dash, her heart in her eyes. He held her gaze for a couple of seconds and then put the car in reverse.

Ashley's spirits sank. Without a backward glance, Dash headed toward the side road that would lead him back to the freeway.

Chapter Five

Ashley watched as Dash and the rental car disappeared from sight. Her heart was in her throat. It was all she could do not to slap her forehead for being so stubborn. But she wasn't the only one. Dash had been stubborn, too. They'd both behaved irrationally, butting heads, letting pride get in their way. Either one of them could have put an end to this stupidity at any time, but they hadn't.

Now it was too late and she was stuck.

Ashley had assumed they were getting along just fine—in fact, better than fine. Until Dash realized he'd lost his phone he'd been a great traveling companion. She'd actually felt a connection to him and had enjoyed herself, which made it all the more difficult to understand why he would be so hardheaded when it came to letting her take the puppy. Even now she was convinced that if he'd done as she suggested and looked at the sweet dog, he'd have given in and changed his mind.

Now here she was, stuck miles from anywhere, alone, desperate, and with a limited amount of cash and no ATM in sight. To make matters worse, all she'd had to eat since the night before was a squished protein bar. Any boost it'd given her had long since worn off. The only food available at the rest stop were stale cookies and a soda machine.

"Miss?" the veteran called out to her from the coffee stand.

Time to put on her big-girl pants, Ashley decided. She straightened and wheeled her suitcase toward the small structure. Seeing that this puppy had already cost her the free ride to Seattle, she wasn't about to let him go now.

"What happened?" the vet asked, eyeing her suitcase.

"Well . . . it turns out my ride wasn't keen on taking the puppy."

"Oh my." The older man's eyes widened when he saw her suitcase. "Is there anyone you can call?"

Ashley shook her head. "No." Her voice wobbled with her answer. "How far are we to the closest town?"

"A ways . . . about thirty miles. My replacement will arrive in a couple of hours and I'd be happy to drive you into town, but the fact is there isn't much there."

"Could I rent a car?" she asked, her eyes full of hope. Then she remembered that was impossible because she wasn't twenty-five.

He scratched his chin and shook his head. "Nothing like that for another hundred, maybe two hundred, miles."

"Oh." Her one hope was to find someone willing to offer her a ride, but the prospect of getting in a car with another stranger intimidated her. A trucker might be willing to help. They were said to be friendly and helpful . . . perhaps a little too friendly, though. Her mother would go ballistic if she learned that Ashley had considered taking such a risk.

"What about a bus stop?" Greyhound made stops in out-of-the-way locations; she just might be in luck.

"Nope."

"Train?" She was getting more desperate by the minute.

He sadly shook his head. "Nothing like that, either. No passenger trains to speak of. Freight trains run regularly, but nowhere close to us."

"Oh." She couldn't hide the defeat in her voice.

"Sorry," he murmured.

She exhaled a deep sigh. "It's not your fault. I brought this on myself."

Ashley collected the puppy and held him close to her chin as she reassessed her options, which seemed to be shockingly few. She didn't know why she'd been so insistent and stubborn. Normally she was far more reasonable. Dash hadn't been any better. The bottom line, she realized, was that she'd wanted Dash to like her, to enjoy her company because she'd enjoyed his. She took it personally that he hadn't felt the same way about her.

Using her suitcase for a chair, she sat on it and waited, although she wasn't exactly sure what she expected would happen. She hadn't been sitting for more than five or ten minutes when she heard the distant rumble of motorcycles. A lot of motorcycles.

Sure enough, ten to fifteen bikes roared into the rest area with the sound equivalent of jet engines.

Ashley's heart started to pound at the sight of the heavily tattooed, muscular men in their leather jackets and helmets. Not one of them seemed to be under six feet tall. They looked rough and mean, exposed to the elements as if the wind and cold couldn't touch them. They backed into the parking spaces and cut their engines. Climbing off their bikes, they looked directly at Ashley. Her mouth went dry. Glancing over her shoulder, she looked toward the war vet and the coffee stand, wondering how much help he'd be if she ran into trouble.

Instead of walking toward the men's restroom, one of

the bikers strolled directly toward her. Not knowing what else to do, Ashley pasted on a smile that trembled at the corners of her mouth and said, "Merry Christmas." Although in her nervousness it came out sounding like "Ferry Just Miss."

"You lost, little girl?" the tattooed biker asked. He had a deep red scar that ran down the left side of his face. He wasn't the kind of man you'd look forward to meeting in a dark alley. The name on his cut said he was called Blade. Ashley didn't need to guess how he'd gotten the name.

"No . . . I'm not lost," she insisted.

"What are you doing sitting here in the cold, then?"

She thought fast. "I'm waiting for my father, the sheriff."

He laughed outright, the sound rusty and gravelly. "Good one. The sheriff here is Elaine Pitman."

"Oh." Ashley offered a weak, apologetic smile. Apparently, he was well acquainted with law enforcement, and she didn't assume it was on a social basis.

A woman with spiky bleached-blond hair stepped up next to Blade and leaned against him. Her body language said she'd look forward to clawing Ashley's eyes out if she even thought about making a move to steal her man. Ashley released an involuntary gasp of fear, wanting to reassure the other woman that she had no intention of flirting with Blade. The blonde's eyes were hard and humorless as she studied Ashley as if she were a piece of litter dirtying the landscape.

The woman nodded toward the restroom and headed in that direction. For half a second Ashley thought she was gesturing for her to follow. She didn't, and it was a good thing, because she soon realized this was the biker chick's way of letting Blade know where she was headed. Ashley looked over her shoulder and saw PROPERTY OF BLADE written across the back of the woman's leather jacket.

"That your puppy?" Blade asked.

Ashley tightened her grip on the dog and nodded, glancing over to see a white car pull into the rest area. She stood. "I think that's my ride now," she said, hoping that would be enough to send the biker on his way.

It wasn't.

The rental car was white, but the world was full of white vehicles, so she didn't dare hope that it was Dash returning. As the car came closer her heart did a little jog of joy.

It *was* Dash. He didn't look happy about it, either. His gaze captured hers and narrowed as he pulled into the empty parking space directly in front of her. She watched as he shifted his attention from her to Blade and the long row of Harleys.

Blade crossed his bulging muscular arms over his equally muscular chest as Dash climbed out of the car. The two men eyed each other warily.

"She your woman?" Blade asked.

Dash snorted as if the very idea was laughable. "No way."

Stung by his denial, Ashley's mouth fell open. She stiffened, and by the sheer force of her will looked away. "He's nothing to me, either," she snapped.

They were at a standoff until Dash finally said, "You coming or not?"

Ashley leaped up so fast her suitcase toppled over.

He smiled and it was all she could do to throw a one-armed hug around him while holding the puppy in the other. "I am so happy to see you."

"Yeah, that was pretty stupid on both our parts."

"You ready to take it back?" she asked, teasing him. "Because if you will, I will."

"I will if you will first," he joked back.

The biker looked from one to the other and glared at them as though they'd spoken a foreign language. "What's with you two? Grow up. You sound like you're in grade school."

Ashley and Dash both laughed. Basically, that was the way they'd behaved.

Dash carried her suitcase to the car and was putting it in the trunk when she asked, "Can I bring Little Blade?"

"Little Blade?"

The biker leveled his chin toward Dash. "Good name for

a dog." He petted the puppy and then opened the passenger door for Ashley, who slipped inside.

"Yes, I named him after my friend here. Blade, meet Dash." Dash looked from her to the biker and then back again.

"Very clever, Ash," he said and rolled his eyes, but he didn't look upset. He just got into the car beside her and turned on the ignition.

Then he did something completely unexpected. He laughed. "You're a devious one." Shaking his head, he put the car in gear and backed out of the space, heading toward the freeway.

"I can't tell you how relieved I am to see you. Thank you."

"I didn't go far before I realized what I'd done. You were right. I was upset about my phone and I took my frustration out on you. As soon as I could find a spot on the freeway to turn around, I did. I'm sorry it took so long."

With the heater blowing, it didn't take Ashley long to warm up. "I noticed you had no problem telling Blade I wasn't your woman," she said, half teasing.

Grinning, he glanced at her. "Count your blessings. For half a second there I was tempted to tell your biker friend that I'd never seen you before in my life."

"But you didn't."

"No, but I probably should have."

Ashley knew he was teasing and the easy banter continued. Little Blade snuggled up in her lap and placed his chin on her thigh and promptly went to sleep. Ashley continued to pet him and was pleased when Dash leaned over and stroked his head, too.

"Are you sure your mom wants another dog?"

"Yeah. She mentioned it recently. It's been a while since she's had a puppy, and knowing my mother, she'll probably spoil him."

"That's what mothers do."

"Speaking of mothers, I really like yours."

"You've never met her," Dash countered.

"I've talked to her, though, and I liked her."

In response he did that thing with his eyes again where he looked toward the heavens.

"Do you know you roll your eyes a lot?" she asked.

"I didn't before I met you."

"Are you trying to say that I frustrate you?" She stopped short of reminding him of what happened the last time he made a derogatory comment about her.

"I'm not trying to say it; I am saying it." He took his eyes off the road long enough to glance her way. "Are you insulted enough to demand that I drop you off at the closest exit?" he asked with a laugh.

"No." The warm feeling continued, and it didn't have anything to do with the inside car temperature. She liked

Dash, and her feelings for him had risen several levels since he came back for her.

"Good thing, because I'd like to reach Seattle some time this year and we won't if we continue with this craziness."

Ashley studied him for a couple of minutes. "You're hungry again, aren't you?"

"What?"

"Like I said earlier, you get cranky when you're hungry."

"I. Am. Not. Cranky." He put emphasis on each word.

She noticed that he didn't deny that he was hungry. "I'm hungry, too, and so is Little Blade. Let's grab a bite to eat."

"Ashley," he complained, exhaling. "I'd like to get as far as we can before the storm hits. We've already wasted an hour."

"We need to eat," she argued. "Okay, I'll tell you what. When we gas up, make sure it's someplace where we can buy sandwiches. We can eat those in the car. I'll buy, just so you know how much I appreciate you coming back for me."

He nodded. "Fair enough."

"See," she said, content now, relaxing against the seat, "I can be reasonable and accommodating and pleasant."

He nodded and his eyes grew slightly darker. "Yes, you can."

"Whoa," she said, and held up her hand. "Was that a compliment?"

For a minute it looked as if Dash was going to deny it. "It might have been."

She planted her hand over her heart. "Careful, you could make a girl faint with that kind of flattery."

His grin grew.

"How soon before we need to get gas?" she asked, when her stomach growled.

"We're down to a quarter tank," he said, and sounded surprised.

That pleased her. "Good."

"No worries, Little Blade," she whispered to the puppy. "Lunch is on the way."

Agent Buckley had the morning-shift reservation clerks from the rental car agencies assembled before Agent Jordan Wilkes entered the private room.

"We appreciate you returning to the airport. I know this is an inconvenience. As you might have guessed, this is a matter of national security. We're hoping you can identify either this man or this woman. There is a possibility they rented a vehicle at the airport earlier today."

He stepped over to the computer screen and pulled up the photo of Ashley Davison, although he didn't hold out much hope that anyone would be able to identify her from the blurry photograph. Looking around the room, all he got were blank stares.

"I might have seen a woman who sort of resembles the photograph," one of the men said. "I helped someone who wore the same colored coat, but the woman in the photograph looks taller and thinner."

"Was she alone?" Agent Wilkes asked.

"She was, and then was later joined by someone else."

"Man or woman?" He snapped the question.

"Man."

Wilkes looked toward Agent Buckley and the hair on the back of his neck rose. This often happened when he felt he was getting close to solving a case. He'd been after Davison for two years; she'd managed to elude him every time. He was determined not to let her escape again. The agency had been unable to get a good likeness. She was a master of disguise and knew how to avoid security cameras.

"Was this the man?" Agent Wilkes clicked a second photograph onto the screen and the much clearer image showed.

"Yes," the car rental clerk answered enthusiastically. "That's him."

"Do you have his name?"

"It's on the rental agreement."

"Your name is?"

"John. John Palmer."

"Can you get the necessary information for us?"

"Yes." He led the way out of the room and to the car rental desk in the bottom level of the airport. The reservation clerk currently on duty moved aside while John Palmer stepped up to the computer and clicked his fingers over the keyboard. Smiling, he looked up. "His name is Dash. Dashiell Sutherland."

"You mentioned earlier that the two didn't appear to be together and then they did."

"Yes, seeing that they were headed in the same direction, they decided to share the car. It was the last one available."

Wilkes leaned toward his partner and whispered, "They might have done this for show, to throw us off. I'd bet my Christmas bonus the two of them are working together."

"We don't get Christmas bonuses," Buckley reminded him.

"If we did, I'd wager mine."

Wilkes returned his attention to the agent. "Did he by chance happen to list his phone number?"

"Yes, it's required." John reached for a scrap piece of paper and wrote down the cell number before handing it to Wilkes.

"Thank you. You've been a great help. Leave your contact information with Agent Buckley and we'll be in touch if we need any further information."

"Glad to help. Will there be anything on the national news about this if you do happen to catch these terrorists?"

"No one used the term *terrorists,*" Agent Wilkes informed him in a stern voice. He didn't want this information leaked when he was only hours away from capturing one of the FBI's Ten Most Wanted.

As soon as they were in a secure area, Wilkes tried the cellphone, which went directly to voicemail.

"Davison might be using Dashiell Sutherland as a pawn. He could be completely unaware of who she is and the danger he's in," Agent Buckley suggested.

"You could be right. I've studied this woman, and this is the way she works. It all seems innocent, innocuous. She comes off as a charming, funny, happy-go-lucky kind of gal. America's sweetheart, but beneath the façade is the heart of a killer."

"We're on her tail now."

"She often will do something to let me know she's outsmarted me."

"You mean like using her real name to buy a ticket?" Agent Buckley asked.

"Exactly. She does that to throw me off, thinking I would never head to Seattle. Coming blatantly to the airport was a ploy. She believes that will send me on a wild-goose chase south instead of north."

Agent Buckley frowned. "You're losing me. She tried to

book a ticket to Seattle, wanting us to think she was headed north, when she's actually heading south, but then goes north?"

"Yes, but I'm not fooled. Mark my words, she's heading to Seattle. The woman is diabolical."

Agent Buckley blinked twice. "That's pretty convoluted thinking, isn't it?"

"That's the way her mind works, which has made it nearly impossible to apprehend her."

As Wilkes spoke he led the way to the rental car lot. He had the location of the vehicle Sutherland had rented, and the make and model of the car, including the license plate number. The garage was mostly empty.

"Do you see anything out of the ordinary?" Wilkes asked the junior agent.

Agent Buckley glanced around and then walked about ten feet away before squatting down.

"What is it?" Wilkes demanded, his heart racing.

Withdrawing a pair of rubber gloves from his pocket, Agent Buckley retrieved a smashed cellphone. "I believe I know why Dashiell Sutherland's cell went straight to voice-mail," he said, holding up the damaged phone. "It looks like a car ran over it." The junior agent looked pleased with himself. "We could assume Davison has taken a hostage. At this point, I wonder if he even knows it."

Chapter Six

Dash and Ashley stopped at the next exit, and instead of gassing up at the station nearest the exit Dash drove two or three miles farther to one with a mini-mart attached. Ashley purchased sandwiches, chips, and drinks for them both while Dash filled the tank.

"I hope you like turkey," she said, when she handed him the cellophane-wrapped sandwich. The only other choice was tuna and she couldn't tolerate even the smell of tuna. Instead, she'd purchased them both turkey with tomato and lettuce instead. And she'd had to dig for those. "I hope you're not a fan of tuna."

Dash cringed. "I never liked canned fish."

"Me, neither."

They sat in the car and Dash peeled off the sandwich wrapping and peeked under the bread. "Turkey with tomato and lettuce," he said, and sounded pleased.

"It's one of my favorites," she commented, peeling away her own wrapping.

"Mine, too." He paused and glanced at her. "I'll admit Little Blade hasn't been a hassle."

Ashley relaxed against the back of the seat and pulled out a small bit of her turkey from the sandwich and fed it to the puppy.

"Aren't you going to say 'I told you so'?" he asked skeptically.

"No. First off, it's early in the trip and I don't want to jinx anything, and second . . ."

"Second," he pressed.

"I think a lot more of you for admitting you were wrong. You didn't need to and you did. That tells me you're not a man with a high sense of self-importance." She'd met more than one of those types and had come to recognize the trait quickly enough.

"So you're into me?"

Although the question was meant as a tease, she sensed he was curious about her feelings for him. There was definitely more than a hint of sexual attraction between them.

She felt it and was certain Dash did, too. Every now and then she'd chance a look at him while he was driving and feel a zing in the pit of her stomach. He'd come back for her at the rest stop, which had earned him enough points to place him in the her-kind-of-hero category.

Without explanation, Dash got out of the car and walked inside the mini-mart.

Taken aback by his abrupt departure, Ashley petted Little Blade and continued to feed him part of her sandwich. Dash was gone less than five minutes, and when he returned he had a large bag in his hand.

"What's that?" she asked, when he set it inside the car on the backseat.

"Puppy food. You don't want to get Little Blade hooked on people food. It's not good for him."

"You bought him dog food?" She hadn't thought to look for it while inside. Dash was right, Little Blade would need the proper nourishment. "That was sweet of you." Thoughtful, too. She was grateful they'd agreed to share the car and the ride. It would have been a long, lonely drive if she'd been alone.

He frowned as if he found her praise disconcerting. "Don't go all mushy on me."

"I'm not," she insisted, but she had and it was useless to deny it. "Come on, say it: You like Little Blade."

Dash shrugged, but reached over and rubbed the puppy's head. "I'll admit he's a cuddly little thing. I can see why you wanted to adopt him."

This was yet another opportunity to tell him she was right. If he'd done as she'd suggested and gone to see the puppy they could have avoided the craziness that followed.

Dash's gaze narrowed. "Stop," he insisted brusquely.

"Stop what?"

"Looking at me like I'm some white knight—I'm not."

"I'd disagree, but it would lead to another senseless argument."

"Yes, it would. I'm no hero, so don't go thinking I'm the kind of guy who'd rush into a burning building to rescue you and Little Blade."

She suspected he would, but again she wasn't going to argue. Instead, she changed the subject completely. "I better take Little Blade out so he can do his business before we leave."

"Good idea."

She climbed out of the car and took Little Blade over to a grassy area and set him down. The puppy went about sniffing every single inch of grass while Ashley whispered encouragement.

"You can do it. Don't you smell where other dogs have been? See how this grass needs watering? That's your job and you need to take it seriously."

Dash got out of the car. "What's taking so long?"

Ashley turned to answer. "He's sniffing the grass."

"Tell him to hurry."

"You tell him," she shouted back, hands on her hips. Of all the ridiculous suggestions! How was an eight-week-old puppy supposed to understand anything yet? Every good thought she'd entertained about Dash flew out the proverbial window. The man had no patience. Surely he realized these things took time.

Dash didn't roll his eyes. Instead, he threw back his head and glared up at the sky.

"Do something" was his next useless suggestion.

"What would you like me to do? Pull down my pants and show him what I want him to do?" she yelled back. "Little Blade is a boy. You show him, and be sure to lift your leg."

Dash muttered under his breath and stalked across the parking lot to where she stood. He looked down the grassy incline and then back at her. "Where is he?" he demanded.

"What do you mean?" Ashley whirled around, and sure enough, Little Blade was missing. "He was here just a minute ago." Her voice rose an entire octave in her panic.

"He couldn't have gone far," Dash insisted.

A chain-link fence separated the mini-mart from a recently plowed field. Checking out the field, Ashley saw movement as Little Blade scrambled over one mound and disappeared behind another. "There," she cried, pointing in the direction of where she'd caught sight of him.

"This is just perfect," Dash said, shaking his head.

"How'd he get over there?" she wondered aloud.

"He didn't get over the fence," Dash commented wryly. "He went under it."

Which, of course, was what had happened.

"Don't worry, I'll get him," she promised. "Little Blade is my responsibility."

Dash folded his arms over his chest. "This I've got to see."

Having something to prove now, Ashley walked across the grass to the chain-link fence and placed the toe of her shoe in the diamond-shaped spaces created by the wire. Next she stretched her arms up as far as they would go and grabbed hold. This wasn't as easy as it looked, but she wasn't about to admit it. She actually was able to make a move, but then lost her footing and was left dangling while she desperately clung to the fence. Her feet started to swing, but she refused to let go, although it was killing her to hang on. Pain shot up her fingers.

"Let go," Dash said, wrapping his arms around her waist.

"But Little Blade—"

"I'll get him," Dash said calmly.

Ashley released her death grip and allowed Dash to

bring her down. He set her on the grass and she turned to thank him. The words caught in her throat as their gazes met and held for the longest moment. Her breathing went shallow and she suspected his did, too. She wanted to say something and found she couldn't. Her throat had closed up and all she seemed capable of doing was staring into his eyes.

He seemed to be experiencing the same things, because he didn't move, either. The attraction sizzled between them. This was happening way too fast. She hadn't felt this strongly about anyone so quickly in, well . . . forever. For a moment it looked as if he intended to kiss her. The truth was she would have let him.

Reluctantly, he loosened his grip. Stepping back, ready to deny what had passed between them if necessary, she brushed the grit from her hands.

Frowning, he shook his head ever so slightly and headed for the parking lot.

Ashley was about to protest when he turned and took a running start toward the fence. He leaped onto the wire and bounded up. In a little more than two moves he was over the fence, landing on the other side in a squatting position.

Within a matter of minutes he'd collected Little Blade. He handed the puppy to her through the space where the dog had gone under the fence and then climbed back over as effortlessly as if he were climbing a ladder.

"That was a bad dog," she whispered in the puppy's ear. "You can't go running off like that, understand?"

"Can we get back on the road now?" Dash asked impatiently, looking pointedly at his watch. "At this rate we aren't going to be able to drive straight through. It's already after three and we haven't gone more than two hundred and fifty miles."

"We can do it." She hoped she sounded optimistic, but she had to admit he was probably right. With the puppy and other necessary stops it would take under twenty-four hours to make the drive. While that still gave him time to make the interview, it was going to be close. She and Little Blade were the ones slowing him down, and Ashley felt bad about that.

They climbed back into the car and she saw that Dash had made a soft bed for Little Blade with a sweater in the backseat. After his run for freedom, the puppy curled up on the sweater and promptly fell asleep.

Ashley waited until they were back on the road before she spoke. "Thank you, again."

"No problem."

"That isn't what you said earlier," she reminded him sheepishly.

"I'd hoped to make better time."

"I know, and it's my fault."

Dash glanced over his shoulder at the sleeping puppy. "You had an accomplice."

"But he's cuddly and cute."

"Both of you are."

His whispered voice was so low that Ashley was sure she was mistaken. "Did you say something?"

"Nothing important," he muttered, seemingly eager to drop the subject.

Ashley decided not to force him to admit what he'd said, but she was fairly certain she'd heard him correctly. Knowing that made her feel warm inside. Nestling in her seat, she leaned her head against the passenger window.

"Mom is going to be so excited to see me," she said, thinking out loud. Already she could picture the way her mother's face would light up when Ashley walked in the door.

"Don't you think you should let her know?"

"No." What was he thinking? "That would ruin the surprise."

"What if she's made other plans for Christmas? Are you sure she intends to sit at home alone, miserable without you?"

"She would be miserable without me. This would have been our first Christmas apart since the day I was born. It was killing us both."

"Maybe she has a boyfriend."

An interesting thought. Ashley needed to think about that and decided it would be a good thing. "I hope she does. My mother is far too wonderful to remain alone the rest of her life. It was hard for me to leave her for graduate school. I know she'd rather have me continue on at the University of Washington. It was hard to leave her, especially knowing how lonely she was after my dad died."

"Maybe you leaving was what she needed."

"How do you mean?"

"She might have grown too content in her comfort zone. With you away at school, she'll be forced to reach out and become more involved in life, meet new people, that sort of thing."

Ashley hadn't thought of it that way. "That's why you suggested Mom might have a love interest." Her mother hadn't mentioned anyone, but then she might feel a bit shy telling her about another man. What Dash said made sense.

"My mother dated some, but she's never gotten serious about another man," he said.

"Your mom's a widow, too?" He hadn't said anything about that earlier.

"Yes."

Here was another something they had in common.

"I remember my first Christmas away from home and family," Dash said, staring straight ahead. "I was in Afghanistan. From the time I could remember I'd always looked forward to Christmas. My mother loves to bake and the holidays give her an excuse to make dozens upon dozens of cookies. My favorites are these little round balls with nuts that she rolls in powdered sugar. I could eat a dozen in one sitting."

"I love those, too. My family calls them Mexican wedding cakes."

He glanced at her and smiled. "But as Christmas approached during my tour in Afghanistan, I dreaded it. All I could think about was everything I was missing at home." He paused and shook his head as though to clear his thoughts. "Funny, I've never mentioned this to anyone else."

"Why not?"

"No reason, I guess. No need to point it out when I was in the service. Everyone in Afghanistan was away from home and loved ones. We made the best of it. The cooks did what they could to create a great meal, but it wasn't the same. Most of us made an effort to be cheerful, but deep down there wasn't a one of us that wouldn't have given just about anything to be home with our family and friends."

By comparison, Ashley was feeling shallow. Dash had been half a world away while she was only a few hundred miles. He'd been in a battle zone and she was in graduate school.

"Even worse, my birthday is the twentieth, so I missed Christmas and my birthday."

Ashley sat up straighter. "You have a December birthday? Get outta here."

"You, too?" He held her gaze a bit longer this time, as if even he felt this strange connection between them.

"The nineteenth."

"That's crazy," he said.

"It is crazy. Did you have relatives who gave you combination gifts—Christmas and birthday?"

"Yes, and it was the pits, especially when I was younger. I used to feel cheated, so my mother threw me half-birthdays in June. She served half a cake with half a scoop of ice cream. She set half the table. Everything was done in halves. It was really fun. My school friends all wanted to come to my half-parties."

"What a wonderful idea." Ashley had already decided that she liked his mother, and this gave her even more reason to do so. She loved the inventive way she'd made Dash's birthday special.

The air between them seemed to be filled with static electricity. Ashley was convinced if she were to reach out and touch him she'd get an electrical jolt. The silence didn't help. She was the one to breach it.

"You think with everything we're finding in common that we could be friends?"

Dash grinned. "You'd think."

"I'm willing."

"I'll think about it."

"Dash!" She punched his arm and he laughed. It wasn't the first time she'd heard him laugh, but there was a difference in him now. He was more relaxed and it felt as if he'd lowered a wall and had come to trust her enough to be willing to share part of himself.

"You should laugh like that more often," she said, wanting him to know she felt more relaxed and at ease with him, too.

"Hey, Ash, are you falling for me?" he asked, teasing her.

"You wish," she said, hiding a smile.

Chapter Seven

Agent Jordan Wilkes rode in the unmarked black Suburban heading north on Interstate 5. A sense of urgency filled him. He was taking a gamble, following the instincts and past experience he'd garnered in pursuit of Ashley Davison. She'd been on his caseload ever since the domestic incident six years ago. She was clever and devious, and Wilkes was determined to see her behind bars before he retired.

Davison had tricked him before, but he'd learned to adjust to her convoluted thinking. He felt sure that she intended to take her hostage to Seattle. By now the former army intelligence officer would most likely have figured out his plight. Wilkes hoped Sutherland would leave clues the FBI could pick up on to aid in his release, before it was too late.

Agent Buckley drove as Wilkes reviewed the collected information regarding Dashiell Sutherland.

"Army intelligence officer," he murmured aloud, as the scenery rushed past. They had given up following the speed limit. Law enforcement would be able to detect that they were government agents and wouldn't pull them over for fudging with the law.

"That's good, right?" Agent Buckley questioned. "That means her hostage is trained. He'd know how to handle this sort of situation. Do you think he was a random captive, or was this prearranged?"

"He worked with intelligence, on the guidance system in drones. I'm guessing she had him pegged. His capture wasn't random. Whatever she's up to, she needs him. The woman may come off as sweet and endearing, but her heart is as black as they come."

Buckley frowned, as if he had a hard time assimilating this information.

Wilkes scowled at the junior agent. "Don't underestimate this woman, Buckley. Her hostage is in serious danger. All we can hope is that we're able to rescue him before she gets what she needs from him."

Wilkes's cell beeped, indicating he'd received a text. Reaching for his phone, he read the message as a sense of satisfaction filled him. "Just as I suspected. Their vehicle was caught on a surveillance camera heading north. They stopped at a rest stop at milepost 451. We might be able to get more information there."

"Heading there now."

A half-hour later they pulled into the rest area. Looking around, the first thing Wilkes noticed was a free coffee stand manned by the local VFW. The man in the booth wore a cap that identified him as a Vietnam vet. If luck was with them, the veteran might be able to provide vital information.

Once Buckley had parked the vehicle, he climbed out and headed toward the booth.

The vet regarded him closely as Wilkes approached. "Can I interest you in coffee?" he asked.

Wilkes flashed his identification. "Can you answer a few questions?"

The vet straightened. "Sure. What do you need to know?"

Agent Wilkes held out a photo of Dashiell Sutherland, taken in the airport. He'd had it blown up to show his face. "Did this man happen to stop here?"

The vet's eyes widened as he studied the photo. "Yes, but I only saw him from a distance."

Wilkes knew it. He'd felt it in his bones. "Was he traveling with anyone?"

"A woman. What's the problem?"

Wilkes ignored the question. "What can you tell me about them?"

The vet shrugged. "Not much . . . well, other than the fact that they had some kind of tiff."

Wilkes looked to Buckley. It was as he suspected. Sutherland wasn't making this easy. Sounded like his training was serving him well.

"Nice gal," the vet continued. "Got a real soft spot for animals. She took my last puppy."

Wilkes frowned. This made no sense. "A puppy?"

"Yes. I found a litter abandoned here when I arrived earlier today and was determined to find homes for the poor little buggers." He looked pleased with himself. "Got homes for them all, too."

Wilkes would need to analyze the reason for the dog. It didn't add up, but then little about this woman did. "Did you see the couple leave?"

The question appeared to unsettle the older man. "Yes and no."

"Explain yourself." Wilkes needed information and he needed it to be clear.

"The man, the one in the photograph, left first without the woman. He wasn't keen on taking the puppy and they had some sort of disagreement."

"An altercation?"

"I guess you could call it that. He drove off without her."

Buckley moved closer and whispered, "Maybe he isn't a hostage after all."

"Possible," Wilkes agreed, but he had to assume that the man had been an innocent bystander—otherwise, the cellphone wouldn't have been destroyed. Then again, the smartphone would have made identifying their location far easier. Davison wasn't dumb enough to keep anything on her person that would pinpoint her whereabouts.

"She sat with the puppy until the motorcycle club showed."

Wilkes straightened. "A motorcycle gang?"

"Large group. Known as the Desperados," the vet clarified. "People around these parts know not to mess with them. It's been a longtime suspicion that they run drugs and guns, but they've never been arrested."

Wilkes knew these gangs often paid off law enforcement. "Did the woman connect with the gang?"

"Must have."

"What do you mean?"

"I couldn't see much from where I was sitting, but I saw her talking to one of the bikers. Don't know his name, and I wasn't looking for any introduction, if you know what I mean."

"We do," Wilkes assured him. "What you did see?"

"Not much, just the two of them chatting, friendly-like.

Then the man you asked me about, he returned and looked real sorry."

"Sorry?"

"Regretful, you know. He loaded up her suitcase and they took off along with the dog."

"What happened to the bikers?"

"Shortly afterward they loaded up and rode out, too."

Confused now, Wilkes absorbed this information. He knew Davison had ties with the underworld—the Mafia, drug cartels, and others. That she'd connect with a motor-cycle gang didn't surprise him. The question that remained was why.

"It was a scheduled meet," he said aloud.

"Say again?" Buckley said, reaching for one of the cook-ies and a cup of coffee.

"She planned the hookup," he repeated, and then looked again at the veteran. "Anything else you can tell us?"

The older man shook his head. "She in some kind of trouble?"

"Anything else?" Wilkes repeated.

"I can't believe that woman is any criminal. She's got a big heart. As soon as she saw the puppy it was like she melted. She talked about her mother and how her dog, Pickles, had died earlier in the year."

"Classic," Wilkes mumbled to the junior agent, turning away and walking toward the parking lot. "She could talk

Santa out of one of his reindeer. The woman comes off as sweet as Christmas fudge, but beneath all that sugar is the heart of a killer."

"What do you make of the motorcycle gang?" Buckley asked.

He was convinced beyond a shadow of a doubt that Davison had scheduled the rendezvous with the gang. "It was planned in advance."

"For what purpose?"

The junior agent was new to the bureau and had a lot to learn. "You remember a few years back a man carrying a bomb was arrested at the Canadian border?"

"Yea, it was big news. He planned on setting it off in the middle of the New Year's celebration at the Seattle Space Needle. You think . . . ?"

"It's a possibility, and my guess is the bikers delivered part of the package."

"You mean a bomb?"

Wilkes nodded. "Makes sense. Seattle has the second-largest New Year's gathering outside of Times Square. Like I said, this wouldn't be the first time the Space Needle has been a target." A new sense of urgency filled him. It was more important than ever that they find Ashley Davison before her plan succeeded.

"I have a question," Buckley said.

"Sure." They climbed back into the car.

"What about the puppy? Why would she take the dog?"

Wilkes had wondered the same thing, but then it came to him in vivid clarity and he bit down hard on his jaw. "I don't even want to say what I think it might mean."

"Tell me," Agent Buckley insisted.

"Trust me, Buckley, you don't want to know."

"Sick bastards," Buckley mumbled.

"I couldn't have said it better myself."

Chapter Eight

"So," Ashley said, paying an inordinate amount of attention to her fingernails, checking her cuticles. "When I spoke to your mother, she said you aren't currently involved in a relationship."

"I believe I was the one who told you that, but only because you insisted on knowing if I was married or involved."

"No, I didn't," she argued, embarrassed when she realized she might have, though purely for practical purposes.

"As I recall, you took one look at me and sized me up as a serial killer."

"Oh, that," she said, and had to admit he was right. "I

was only being cautious. A girl can't be too careful these days." She watched *20/20* and *Dateline* religiously.

He made a low scoffing sound. "Do you feel safer now?"

"I suppose." She made an effort to sound offhanded, as though she hadn't completely made up her mind. Basically, she had. Dash had proven he could be trusted. It wasn't every guy who would leap over a fence to rescue a puppy, and that wasn't all. This guy had gone above and beyond in every way. More and more she found herself grateful they were sharing the ride. She enjoyed his company and she felt safe with him. Protected. Besides, he was fun, and the banter between them kept her entertained.

Dash didn't say anything for a few minutes, but Ashley could tell something was on his mind by the way his fingers tapped against the steering wheel.

"What exactly did my mother tell you?" he asked in a disinterested sort of way.

Ashley wasn't fooled. "I don't remember," she lied.

"Yes, you do. Just tell me."

"Well, she said that by age thirty she'd given birth to both you and your sister. She also mentioned that she didn't know what it's going to take for you to find a decent girl and settle down."

He snorted softly. "That sounds like my mother."

"She blames the army."

"She was against it when I decided to enlist," he mentioned. "A lot of mothers are, and with reason, I suppose."

"Was it a good decision?" Ashley was interested in hearing his side. Although they weren't well acquainted, she didn't think he was the kind of man to make a spur-of-the-moment life decision. She suspected something had led to it. Instinctively, she knew it was a breakup with a woman. She'd once read a story that claimed relationship breakups were the number-one or -two reason men signed up for the armed services.

"It was a good decision for me. I gained a lot of knowledge that's helping me in civilian life. It's why I was chosen for this interview. Besides computer skills, the military taught me discipline and how to work as a team. My unit became as tight as brothers."

"What about people skills?" she asked.

"Are you suggesting I have poor people skills?" He appeared to find the question amusing.

"Not in the least . . . it just seems like a life skill one would acquire as part of the armed forces."

"I'd like to think I did."

"But there was no time for . . . women?"

He attempted to hide a smile, without success. The edges of his mouth quivered with the effort. "What makes you ask?"

His question took her by surprise. She wasn't prepared to answer, but quickly ad-libbed. "Well, it seems, you know, that you would be involved."

"Why's that?"

She might as well say it. It wasn't like Dash didn't know. "You're sort of good-looking . . . I mean, women, other women, not me in particular, tend to notice that in a man."

"They do?"

"Oh come on, Dash, don't be coy. You know the way women look at you, so it only makes sense that you would, you know, look back."

"Yes, I suppose it does, but I was up to my eyeballs in work. I've only been out of the army two months. I enjoyed military life, but I didn't want another tour in Afghanistan, and the handwriting was on the wall."

"You're avoiding the question."

He exhaled. "No, I'm not. While in the service I didn't have time for a serious relationship, and frankly, I wasn't all that interested."

Ashley arched her brows and turned her head to look out the window. It'd started to snow. Just a few flakes, not enough for Dash to turn on the windshield wipers—at least not yet.

"What was that look about?" Dash demanded.

Ashley didn't realize that he'd seen her reaction. "Nothing."

Dash groaned. "I hate it when a woman says that, because it clearly is something. So don't give me that 'it's nothing' crap. I want to know what you're thinking."

"Fine, I'll tell you. We all make time for what's important to us, and clearly a relationship isn't high on your list of priorities."

He took a moment to mull that over. "An interesting observation."

"I'm right, though." She made it a statement and not a question.

"Basically."

She smiled, feeling good that he was willing to admit it. A man of his integrity was a rare find. Ashley found it far too easy to fall for him.

"What's your story?" he asked, turning the tables on her.

"Me?" She pressed her hand against her breast. "We weren't talking about me. Besides, who says I'm not involved?"

"Are you?"

"Not currently," she admitted with some reluctance.

"But you were until recently?"

The falling snow started to thicken. "Sort of," she said, hedging.

"Sort of? What does that mean?"

She wasn't going to be able to escape this inquisition,

and she had no one to blame but herself. She was the one who'd opened this Pandora's box. "It means," she said, inhaling deeply, "I was involved and so was he, but apparently not just with me."

Dash's face broke into an easy smile.

"I don't see why you find this amusing," she muttered. "Trust me, from my point of view it wasn't the least bit funny."

"I bet not. How'd you find out?"

Ashley stiffened. He acted like this was all one big joke. "I'm not telling you that."

"Come on, humor me."

"No way."

"Why not? It's in the past, right?"

"Yes." She shifted in her seat; this conversation was growing uncomfortable.

"You're over him?"

Ashley wasn't sure she wanted to answer that. Her brief relationship with Jackson continued to trouble her. She didn't know how she could have been so blind. "What makes you say that?"

That smile of his was back and wider than ever. "Because you're flirting with me."

The man was infuriating. "I am not flirting with you." She made sure each word was distinctly enunciated.

He laughed outright. "Yes, you are."

Ashley's back went broomstick straight. "Jackson broke my heart."

"Unlikely." His tone was flippant.

Now Dash was getting downright irritating. "When did you become an expert on human emotions? I was devastated. Other than classes and work, I spent hours lying on the floor, sobbing and listening to Adele."

"How long ago did this happen?"

She crossed her arms over her chest and stared straight ahead. "I'm not answering any more of your questions. What happened between Jackson and me is none of your business."

"Your pride was stung, but you didn't really love him."

So he was determined to continue the conversation. "You're not a nice person, Dash." She didn't really believe that, but she wasn't letting him know otherwise.

"We've already established that. Now you know the real reason I'm not in a relationship. I screw it up every time."

Aha! This was promising. "So you've had your own share of heartache."

"*Heartache.* That's a woman's word."

"All right, failed relationships."

"Better. I've had a few."

"Did you cheat?"

"No," he said, as if it was an insult for her to suggest that he would.

"Forget her birthday?"

"M-a-y-b-e." He dragged out the word, making it sound as if he'd consider that a minor infraction.

"Come on," she said, uncrossing her arms and angling her body toward him. "Fess up. Inquiring minds what to know."

"Apparently, women want to spend every waking minute with a guy. I can't stand a clingy woman. Unfortunately, those are the ones who are most drawn to me. I like my space. I need my space," he reiterated. "I don't want to answer twenty text messages a day or make an excuse to have a beer with a friend."

"Is this friend male or female?"

"Male." He tossed her a look that said his answer should have been obvious.

"Okay, continue." She gestured with her hand, wanting more details.

"I don't want a woman to follow me to the tennis courts and watch my match, or just happen to run into me when I'm out. It's too much togetherness. Give me room to breathe."

"What about men?" she challenged. "They have their own set of issues, one of which is finding a way to keep their zipper in the locked position."

"Men's zippers don't lock."

"My point exactly."

He chuckled. "Okay, we can agree men and women each have their own weaknesses."

"What you said about giving a man his space is interesting." She was willing to give him that. "I've known women like that."

"Unfortunately, so have I," he muttered. His hand tightened around the steering wheel, "Something else that really gets me is this incessant need to chatter."

He was on a roll now. Ashley went quiet as she studied him. While his tone made light of the situation, she could see there was more to it.

"What?" he asked. "You're looking at me like I'm Little Blade and you want to pet me."

She smiled. "You're acting like this is a joke, but you were hurt." This would be much harder for him to admit.

He didn't answer for what felt like a long time. "Yeah, I was hurt, but I got over it. You were hurt, too."

She nodded and found she didn't want to talk about her breakup. "And for your information, women don't chatter," she insisted, righteously defending all women.

"Then tell me why they have to discuss every inconsequential detail of their lives and everyone else's lives, too. I don't care who got cut from *Dancing with the Stars,* or which celebrity couples are dating. And I'm up to here"—he paused and made a cutting motion over the top of his head—"with Brad and Angelina. If I wanted to know any of this nonsense, I'd read a tabloid."

"That tells me you're dating shallow women. But I'm guessing they're all really pretty, which also tells me you're ruled by testosterone."

"Excuse me?"

"Okay, I'll put it bluntly: Your brains are located below your belt."

"That's possible."

The snow had started coming down hard now. The car's wiper blades were hardly able to keep up. It'd grown dark and the driving was becoming more hazardous by the minute.

Concerned with the snow, Ashley gasped when the car skidded, nearly going sideways on the slick road. She braced herself, her hand clutching the door.

"It might be a good idea if we stop for the night."

The teasing, fun atmosphere vanished. "What about your interview? It's tomorrow, isn't it?"

"In the afternoon. We'll get an early start and I shouldn't have any trouble making it on time."

Ashley had to agree, driving conditions had become too hazardous to continue.

Chapter Nine

Dash took the next exit off the freeway, but instead of heading toward the row of hotels closest to the off-ramp, he continued down the road.

"Where are you going?" Ashley asked.

"I'm looking for a Walmart or a Target so we can get Little Blade a collar and leash. I don't want a repeat of what happened earlier today."

"Good idea." Mentally, Ashley calculated the amount of cash she had with her. She reached for her purse and counted out her cash.

"I'll pay and you can reimburse me later."

"I'll use my debit card." A warm sensation came over

her and she smiled because "later" meant that he fully intended on seeing her after this trip. While he might not have meant anything by it, his words pleased Ashley.

"Do you want to explain why you're wearing that Cheshire cat smile?" he asked, glancing her way.

"Not really." She was embarrassed that he'd noticed.

"Do it anyway," he insisted.

"Oh all right, if you must know . . ."

"I'm mildly curious."

Liar. He would hound her until he got the truth out of her. And if she was honest with herself, she certainly wouldn't mind seeing him after this trip. "Mildly curious or not, I got the feeling, just now, that we might connect, you know, after Christmas." She sounded nervous and unsure of herself and wished she'd kept her mouth shut.

A smile came and went from his eyes. "Well, duh. We have to get back to San Francisco, don't we?"

Ashley had forgotten about that. "Actually I . . . I'd hoped to fly."

"Good luck with that. In case you've forgotten, this is the holiday season and all the flights are probably booked solid—even after the holidays."

"Right." The thought of returning with Dash wasn't unpleasant. She'd look forward to it. "In that case, I won't mind driving back with you."

"Big of you," he teased.

"If you remember, it didn't start out so great this morning, but I've had a change of heart, seeing that you're so clearly not a serial killer."

Dash snorted. "I might have pulled the wool over your eyes, you never know," he teased, and then added, "Besides, it's clear you think I'm amazing."

"Excuse me?" She exaggerated each word, laughing. "You're delusional, but enjoy it while you can."

"I intend to." Teasing light brightened his eyes. The electricity between them seemed to grow stronger, she noticed, and she hid a smile, thinking how much she was enjoying being with Dash. This morning she would never have guessed it could be possible for them to travel together and for her to like him this much.

As they continued down the road, businesses lined both sides of the street. Ashley kept a watch for a Target or a Walmart, but as she did her mind mulled over the next few days.

"Dash, if I travel back with you, then that means you'll spend Christmas in Seattle, right?"

"Yeah. So?"

"So how would you feel about spending Christmas Day with my mom and me? We'd love to have you, and you aren't going to get a better Christmas dinner. My mother makes the most incredible stuffing." She was talking fast, unsure of why she should feel hesitant and awkward. "Say, do you know the difference between stuffing and dressing? I just learned this." Ashley knew she was chattering, which was something Dash said he disliked, but she couldn't seem to help herself. Dash unnerved her. Worse, she realized it was because she was afraid he would refuse her invitation, and she really wanted him to share Christmas with her and her mother.

"Okay, what's the difference between stuffing and dressing?"

She noticed he didn't say anything about the Christmas invite. "Stuffing is cooked inside of the bird and dressing is cooked outside of the bird. Makes sense, doesn't it?"

"Guess I never thought about it."

"I know. Me, neither." She waited for a moment and then asked again: "About Christmas?"

He hesitated. "I'd be happy to join you, but I'd be more comfortable if you talked to your mother about it first."

"I know my mom, she won't mind."

"Talk to her first," he insisted.

"Okay, I will, but she'll be happy to include you, seeing how crazy you are about me."

He chuckled, and soon she found herself smiling, too, as the unease slowly evaporated.

Ashley spotted a Walmart sign and pointed it out. "Up ahead on the right."

"I see it." Dash stopped at the light and then made a

right-hand turn into the parking lot. A fresh Christmas tree lot took up one side of the asphalt, with multicolored lights strung around the perimeter. The freshly fallen snow weighed down the branches, giving the trees a magical appearance. Ashley loved the scent of fresh trees, but her mother insisted on an artificial one because of the fire hazard.

"You need anything else besides the leash and collar?"

"No . . . do you think it will take long? I hate the thought of leaving Little Blade alone in the car." But he'd be warm enough with the sweater wrapped around him.

"He'll be fine for a few minutes. Once we find a hotel I'll take him out and walk him. Hopefully the snow and the cold will be enough to cause him to hurry and do his business."

"I'll take him out," she said, although she appreciated his offer. It was cold and miserable, and she was the one who'd adopted the puppy, which he was generous enough not to remind her.

The lot was nearly full and it took a few minutes to find a parking space. Unfortunately, it wasn't anywhere close to the store, which meant a long trek through the slushy lot. Thankfully, Ashley had worn her boots. Dash offered his elbow and she gratefully wrapped her arm through his. The lot was icy and slippery, and she would have fallen if not for Dash's hold on her.

"You really are a gentleman," she teased.

"Just keep telling yourself that," he joked back.

Ashley smiled. This was turning out to be a grand adventure, and not only because she was beginning to really like Dash, but because she enjoyed the drive as well. Soon they'd be in Seattle, and she felt a little giddy thinking that wouldn't be the last she'd see of him.

Once inside, Dash grabbed an empty cart.

They passed the sale aisle and right away one of the items caught Ashley's attention. "Dash, look. Peanut butter is on sale." She grabbed a jar and placed it inside the cart.

He regarded her skeptically. "You're buying peanut butter?"

"This stuff is like gold to a grad student. That and Velveeta cheese. I live on peanut butter."

"That explains a great deal," he said, shaking his head, mocking her.

Ashley playfully punched his arm and noticed he was smiling. It was hard to pull her gaze away from him. Harder than it should have been.

Dash expertly wove them down one aisle and to the next until they reached the pet section. "Look at this," she said, pointing out a cute little reindeer band with tiny green and red bells made especially for small dogs.

"No way," Dash said. shaking his head. "You are not going to embarrass Little Blade with that headpiece."

"But . . ."

"Would Big Blade wear that?"

Ashley was well aware that Blade would likely do bodily harm to anyone who so much as approached him with anything so ridiculous. "That's an unfair question."

"Then you know the answer."

"What about a Santa hat? Little Blade is a Christmas gift for my mother, you realize."

Dash refused to answer, and didn't say anything when she added it to the cart. It didn't take her long to decide on the collar and leash, a carrier, and a bag of doggie treats, plus a chew toy.

"You ready to check out?" Dash asked when she'd finished clearing out the pet section.

"Okay."

"You sure you don't want to check to see if Velveeta cheese is on sale?"

"I'm sure." She took out the jar of peanut butter and replaced it on the shelf. It was a bit ridiculous to cart that to Seattle and then back to San Francisco.

"No peanut butter and no Velveeta? You're sure you can make it to Seattle without 'em?" he teased.

Ashley elbowed him in the ribs. Oh yes, she was enjoying Dash's company far and above anything she could have anticipated.

———

"Are they inside the store yet?" Travis McCurry asked, looking to his best friend, Justin Troup.

"Yeah."

"You brought the screwdriver, right?"

"Got it." Justin took it out of his hip pocket and glanced nervously around them. "You sure we won't get caught?"

"I'm sure."

"You've done this before?"

"No," Travis murmured, and despite his best effort, his voice lacked confidence. "My dad would shoot me if he knew what I was doing." Travis's hand trembled as he approached the rear of the vehicle. He'd waited nearly an hour in the cold, sitting in his car and growing impatient, before the right vehicle turned up. It probably wasn't necessary to have the same color and same model car, but he wasn't taking any chances. No one would notice the switch in the license plates as easily, he reasoned, although he had no idea if that was true. It was his fault that he'd gotten into this mess.

"I don't have a choice." In Travis's mind, trading the license plate from this car with his own was his only option.

His grandmother had bought him the car for his seventeenth birthday with the understanding that he would maintain honor-roll grades, which wasn't a problem—he worked hard and he had earned top grades. The one stipulation his parents made was that Travis pay for his own car insurance, gas, and license fees.

Travis had readily agreed. He had a job as a busboy at a local restaurant and the manager liked him. He hoped that by summer he'd get promoted to a server and the tips would be great.

The problem came when he asked Bailey Thompson to the holiday dance. His mom had paid the rental fee for his tuxedo, but then there was the cost to attend the dance and the corsage and pictures and a bunch of other stuff he hadn't counted on, and he'd gone through his savings in less than a week.

The choice was skip either taking Bailey to dinner before the dance or paying the renewal for his car registration. He chose to take Bailey to dinner, which left him driving around town with expired tabs. So far he'd been lucky, but eventually he'd get caught.

By chance Travis saw a news report about people stealing license plates off cars, which gave him the idea. This wasn't exactly stealing, though. All he intended to do was switch plates. The license on the white car he'd spotted had a full nine months left on the tabs. When renewal time came next November . . . well, he hadn't figured that part out yet.

Travis and Justin squatted down behind the car. Travis's hand shook, but it was from nerves more than the cold.

A car horn blared in the distance.

"They're coming," Justin said, and leaping up, he raced around the corner of the store, slip-sliding in the snow in his rush to escape. They hadn't been inside more than ten minutes. Twelve, tops.

Terrified he was about to get caught, Travis fell flat on his backside, cold, wet snow seeping through his jeans. He heard something, too. An inhuman noise. He had one screw left and he wasn't about to run scared now. But he was on a mission, and no matter what, he was determined to finish the task.

Travis peeked around the side of the car and saw a vehicle in the row in front of them backing out of the space. Sighing with relief, Travis realized it wasn't the car owner.

Travis stood and gave Justin the all-clear sign.

In an attempt to look cool, Travis left the security of his hiding spot. He looked both ways before he left the shelter of the building. As he approached the vehicle, the noise returned.

"I hear bells," Justin said in a loud whisper.

"So do I." Travis noticed a volunteer ringing the bell in front of the store, collecting money for charity.

"Don't you care? We could get caught any minute."

"Not really. I'm cool. What about you?"

Shrugging, Justin stuffed his hands in his pockets, belying his earlier behavior. "Yeah, me, too."

"No, you're not." Travis was starting to enjoy this.

"I'm not afraid. Just saying, if we get caught, I'll throw you under the bus so it's your neck and not mine."

"Thanks, dude."

"I'm not going to prison for you because you've got the hots for Bailey Thompson."

A whining noise caught his attention now. Travis frowned. "That sounds like a . . . dog?"

With his hands cupping each side of his face, Justin peered inside the car.

"What is it?" Travis asked.

"It is a dog . . . a puppy."

Travis had the license plate off, so all he needed to do now was replace it with his expired plate. Really, this wasn't nearly as hard as it was at first. Thankfully, they were hidden in the shadows.

Justin continued to peer inside the car. "The puppy's got his paws up against the window. He must be hungry."

"Are the doors locked?"

Justin jumped back, looking horrified. "I'm not getting my fingerprints on the car."

"Wear gloves." As a partner in crime, his best friend had failed big-time. Then again, not getting caught while committing a crime wasn't a subject they learned in school.

"Oh yeah, gloves." Justin pulled a pair out of his coat pocket and slipped them on his hands. Next he tried the door. "It's locked."

"I don't think we have to worry. The dog won't rat us out."

"Good thing."

"You don't see the couple coming back, do you?"

"No," he said, and then in a panicked voice added, "Wait. I think that's them coming out of the store now."

Travis froze. He didn't dare take a chance to stand up and look.

"The woman had on a red coat, right? And knee-high brown boots?"

"Yeah. What about the guy?"

"Hey, she's not bad-looking."

"What about the guy?" Travis repeated.

"He's all right, I guess."

"I'm not asking about his looks."

Justin glanced nervously toward Travis. "You done yet?"

"Almost."

"Hurry."

"I'm going as fast as I can." Travis's hands felt like they were frozen, and because he was close to panicking, he dropped the last screw.

"Distract them," Travis pleaded.

"How?"

"I don't know. Just do it."

"Okay, but you owe me."

Stuffing his hands into his pockets and whistling "Oh, Christmas Tree," Justin sauntered toward the approaching couple.

Travis did everything he could to hurriedly find the screw in the snow and then twist it into place. He couldn't make out his friend's words, but he could hear Justin rattling away in an effort to slow the couple down.

Finished now, Travis stood and tucked the license plate he'd removed inside his winter coat. Casually, he strolled up to Justin.

"I'm sorry, folks, is my friend bothering you?"

"Not at all," the woman said. "He was practicing his lines for a school play and he sounded pretty good."

"Cool. Time to go. Merry Christmas."

"Merry Christmas," the woman said, but the man didn't look nearly as friendly or trusting. In fact, he regarded them suspiciously.

But then Travis was certain he must look guilty as sin. Perhaps because he was.

Chapter Ten

Redding, California, Ashley decided, was a rather nice town, nestled as it was in the thick natural forest of Northern California, with the Sacramento River running through the heart of the city.

Ashley knew Dash would have preferred to keep going, but with the snow, driving over Siskiyou Pass into Oregon it would have been treacherous, especially now that it was dark. He was only being cautious to suggest they spend the night in a hotel.

Depending on how early they started out in the morning, they should be able to safely make it to Seattle by midafternoon. It didn't give Dash a lot of time to spare, but it was workable.

Dash hadn't mentioned much about the job interview, but she knew it was important to him. She remembered how serious he'd been when talking to the reservation clerk at the Highland Airlines desk and later when they'd both wanted the same rental car. He'd insisted it was vital that he be in Seattle on the twenty-second.

No matter what, they had to get to Seattle in time for his interview. Ashley was determined to do everything within her power to make sure that happened.

"Any of these hotels look good to you?" Dash asked, pulling her out of her thoughts. The snow was thicker than ever now, and falling harder by the minute. If Dash had his phone they would have been able to check weather conditions for tomorrow. Unfortunately, her outdated flip phone was no help. A new phone was at the top of her Christmas list.

"Ashley?" he asked again.

"Oh, sorry. Any one will do. You decide." She appreciated his thoughtfulness in asking.

"Okay." He pulled into a well-known reputable chain hotel and parked under the portico. They left Little Blade in the car while they went inside.

"I hope they don't object to puppies," Ashley whispered on their way through the lobby. She knew Little Blade wouldn't be a problem. She'd make sure he spent the night in the carrier.

Dash approached the counter, the corner of which was decorated with a small pot-sized Christmas tree. A few Christmas cards were taped along both sides of the reception desk. The man behind it looked decidedly bored and was fingering a magazine when they approached.

"Happy holidays," Ashley greeted, hoping her smile would convince him she would keep a good watch on the puppy.

"You, too," he responded, and smiled back. He came to attention and reluctantly slid his gaze to Dash.

"Do you have two rooms available?" Dash asked.

"We do. Weather caused a bunch of cancellations, so you're in luck."

"Great." Dash brought out his credit card.

"Is a puppy okay?" Ashley asked, gracing him with a big smile. She leaned closer and asked what he was reading and continued the conversation as if he was the most interesting man she'd ever encountered.

"About the puppy?" Dash ground out the question.

The clerk reluctantly turned his attention away from Ashley to Dash. "No problem, we're animal-friendly. There's a small fee attached."

"Great." Ashley felt as if a weight had been lifted off her shoulders. Dash had been a good sport to this point, but she didn't think his cooperative mood would hold if they were forced to drive from one hotel to another in search of one that would take them plus Little Blade.

Dash paid for his room with a credit card and Ashley paid with hers. Once they filled out the paperwork and collected their room keys, they returned to the car. Dash hadn't looked overly pleased, and he should have been. Not only had they secured two rooms, but the hotel had a restaurant and lounge. They hadn't eaten in hours and she was hungry.

"You hungry again?" she asked, as Dash brought out her suitcase from the trunk of the car. He hadn't said a word to her since they entered the lobby.

He paused and looked at her. "I'm fine; what makes you ask?"

"You seemed a little annoyed back there."

"Annoyed?"

"Yeah. You've been frowning at me and were short-tempered with the guy behind the desk. What gives?"

He held her look for a long moment. "I don't get why you felt you had to flirt."

Ashley was stunned. "You're joking."

"Okay, fine, forget it."

Ashley loved it. Her face broke into a wide smile. "You're jealous!"

He looked at her as if that was the most ludicrous thing she'd ever said. "Get over yourself."

"This is so great," she whispered, pleased as could be.

"What?" Dash demanded.

"I knew you were into me. Told you so."

His dour look melted into a sexy grin. "I'll admit it set me off."

"I was softening him up, hoping he'd tell me Little Blade wouldn't be a problem." She knew it had been disingenuous of her.

Dash finished unloading the trunk while she set a sleepy Little Blade inside his carrier. They each had bottom-floor rooms with sliding glass doors that opened up to the pool area. "I'll take Little Blade outside with his leash."

"While you're doing that, I'll park the car," Dash added.

"As soon as I get Little Blade settled in his carrier, I'll meet you in the restaurant."

Ashley dragged her suitcase and Little Blade to her room. As soon as she was inside, she released the puppy from the carrier and attached his collar. She opened the sliding glass door to take him outside. An inch or two of pristine snow marked the patio, with the outside lights glistening on the snow. Little Blade buried his nose in the cold slush and then shook his head before prancing around the area. When she saw a bright yellow mark, she knew it was time to bring him back inside.

As soon as she placed him inside the carrier, he curled into a ball and went to sleep. They'd been fortunate thus far. Other than that one escape attempt in the field, he'd been a well-behaved puppy.

Next Ashley opened her suitcase and brought out her pajamas and a change of clothes. This outfit was one of her nicest; she wanted to impress Dash, especially since he'd basically admitted he'd been jealous of the guy at the front desk.

By the time she joined him, Dash had a booth in the restaurant. He studied her change of outfits appreciatively but didn't comment. She didn't need him to tell her she looked nice—the way his steady gaze moved over her said as much.

Ashley was beyond hungry and slipped into the seat and reached for the menu. "I could eat everything on the first page," she murmured, reading over the selections.

When the waiter came for their order she couldn't make up her mind and opted for two appetizers instead: French onion soup and a hamburger slider. Dash ordered the day's special, spaghetti and meatballs. The restaurant had only a handful of customers. The lounge looked busier, but it was past the normal dinner time.

Apparently, it was karaoke night, because a disc jockey was whipping up the energy in the room, offering prizes and incentives to the crowd. It wasn't long before Ashley was tapping her foot to the music, listening and appreciating the talent, most of whom appeared to be locals.

"If you start singing I'm outta here," Dash teased.

"Do you sing?" she asked eagerly.

Dash shrugged. "I was in choir in junior high school, but I haven't sung in years."

He was full of surprises. "Me, too, both junior high and high school. Have you done karaoke?"

"No." Just the way he snapped out the word suggested he wasn't interested.

"Come on, Dash. It'll be fun."

He didn't hesitate. "No way."

"You're dying to do it," she said, refusing to believe him. "What you need is some incentive."

"You sign me up and you can walk the rest of the way to Seattle."

"You don't mean that."

"Don't test me, Ash. I'm serious."

She loved it when he called her Ash, but she could see this was an argument she was destined to lose. "Okay, fine."

"I don't want to get within six feet of that lounge, understood?"

"Okay, okay, message received."

"Don't let me stop you, though."

She nodded. Disappointment settled over her. She would like nothing better than the two of them getting on stage and singing together, but clearly that wasn't going to happen. This wasn't going to be a scene from *High School Musical*.

Their food arrived. Ashley ate her way through both appetizers, shocked that she could stuff down that much food in one sitting. She noticed Dash was equally successful in eating everything off his plate.

They chatted amicably through dinner while her foot tapped to the beat. For the most part, the singers were good. It looked like great fun, and after being cooped up in the car all day, Ashley was ready to relax and enjoy the evening, with or without Dash, but she hoped it would be with him.

"Let's get a drink in the lounge," she suggested hopefully, eyeing the other room. She'd enjoyed listening to the singers. Some showed real talent, while others made her grit her teeth.

"You're looking for an excuse to drag me up onstage, aren't you?" Dash accused her.

"I promise I won't force you," she said, batting her eyelashes at him, hoping he'd have a change of heart. She loved karaoke, but it'd been weeks—no, months—since she'd last been onstage. And she wasn't half bad, or so she'd been told.

Dash looked toward the ceiling. "I can't believe I'm agreeing to even sit and listen."

Ashley smiled, the joy of the season nearly overwhelming her. "Other than this morning, I've had a perfectly wonderful day."

Dash reached for her hand. "I wish I could say the same."

"Dash!"

"Okay, okay, you aren't so bad."

Ashley shook her head. "Be careful or your compliments are likely to overwhelm me."

Dash chuckled. "Okay, Taylor Swift, let's check out the lounge."

The bar was hopping and they were fortunate to find a high top, joining another couple who were willing to share. Ashley wasn't much of a drinker, but it generally took at least one alcoholic beverage for her to loosen up enough to sing in front of a crowd.

The waiter came by and Dash ordered a beer, so she asked for a Fuzzy Navel, her favorite. It wasn't an over-the-top drink and the alcohol was easily disguised by the orange juice.

Within minutes the songbook made it in their direction. It didn't take Ashley long to make her selection. But it would be a while before her number came up and she wanted to check on Little Blade.

"I'll be right back," she said, after taking the first sip of her Fuzzy Navel.

Dash nodded, paying close attention to the woman on the stage belting out a Sam Smith song as if giving a Grammy performance. Ashley didn't appreciate his rapt attention on the other woman.

Leaning close, she told him, "I can show signs of jealousy, too, you know."

He grinned as if he found her comment amusing. Ashley wasn't trying to be funny; she was serious. She had no right to feel anything toward Dash. Hours earlier they'd been complete strangers. They hadn't even kissed, but she would have gladly done so if the opportunity arose . . . and she hoped it would.

"I thought you were leaving," he said, looking back at her as though surprised she was still there.

"I was, but I wanted to be sure some hottie didn't steal you away."

With his eyes holding hers he raised his hand and brushed a finger down the side of her face. Ashley held her breath as a wealth of sensation left her nerves tingling. It felt as if his finger had been on fire and spread heat throughout her body. Although his finger only skimmed her face, she felt his touch everywhere.

"No worries there," he whispered.

Ashley reluctantly backed away and hurried to her room to check on Little Blade. The music from the bar followed her. She was concerned that the puppy would be restless in the carrier and want out. Little Blade whined pitifully as soon as she opened the door.

"Oh sweetie," she whispered, her fears realized. Kneeling on the floor next to her open suitcase, she released the door to his small carrier and brought him out. Without invitation he climbed into her lap and stretched upward in order to lick her face. "You're adorable and you know it, don't you?"

She brought Little Blade back down to her lap and petted him and tickled his stomach. "Are you hungry?" Ashley remembered the treats she'd picked up while they were at Walmart and found the sack, sorting through the supplies until she found what she was looking for. She tore open the package and handed him a small bone-shaped goodie, which Little Blade immediately jumped on.

She heard the announcer in the far-off room call out the number for the next singer. Casually, Ashley glanced at the number in her pocket, convinced there must be three or four others ahead of her.

As soon as she realized it was her, she leaped to her feet. "That's me. Oh my goodness . . ." Without thought, she raced out of the room. This was her moment to shine in front of Dash. Her hope was that he'd be so overwhelmed by her extraordinary talent that he wouldn't be able to contain himself.

"I'm here. I'm here," she called out, as she rushed back into the bar.

She made her way to the front and found the disc jockey. "Am I too late?" she asked, placing her hand over her pounding heart. She didn't know she could move that fast.

"You're fine," he assured her, and handed her the microphone.

Ashley climbed the two steps to the small stage and waited for the music to cue up. Her gaze searched the room until she found Dash. She smiled at him and he smiled back and then winked, taking a sip of his beer. She'd had only the one small taste of her own drink, and she grew nervous. A drink usually helped, but one sip wasn't nearly enough and she wanted this song to wow him.

The music started, and with her eyes holding Dash's, she whispered in a husky voice, "Santa, baby . . ."

A small commotion started in the back of the room. Ashley did her best to ignore it. But then the noise and laughter moved forward and several people started to point down toward the floor.

It took only a couple of moments for Ashley to realize the source of their amusement.

Little Blade had followed her into the bar. In her rush she must have left the door partially open. The puppy had escaped and brought something with him.

And it wasn't the bone she'd given him just a few minutes earlier.

Instead, Little Blade happily trotted toward the front of the stage dragging her bra with him.

Chapter Eleven

Ashley was mortified. She leaped down from the stage in order to catch Little Blade, but before she could reach him, a middle-aged man in the audience snagged the bra. As soon as he wrestled it away from Little Blade, he swung it in wide circles above his head like a victory flag.

Ashley was convinced her face had turned purple with humiliation. She managed to grab hold of Little Blade and turned to see Dash standing eye to eye with the man swinging her bra. Dash said something to the other man that caused him to take a step back. Whatever Dash said was effective, because the smile left the other man's face and he willingly handed over Ashley's bra.

With her underwear in hand, Dash joined her. "Are you ready to leave now?" he asked, as if the question was even necessary. Ashley couldn't get out of that lounge fast enough.

"Please." She tucked Little Blade under her arm, and with her head lowered, she nearly ran toward their rooms. As soon as they were out of earshot, she mumbled, "I have never been so embarrassed in my life."

If Dash so much as smiled or cracked a joke, she didn't know what she'd do. "Could I please have my bra back?" she asked, as soon as they turned down the corridor that led to their side-by-side rooms.

He held out her bra, but she could see that he was trying not to laugh.

He might think this was funny, but she definitely didn't. "Don't you dare," she threatened.

"Sorry. If you could have seen the look on your face."

She snatched the bra out of his hand and grabbed her key card, eager to disappear and bury her sorrows in a package of M&M'S from the minibar. This was what she got for her attempt to look sexy and sultry for Dash.

Little Blade squirmed in her arms as she struggled to hold on to him and manage the key card. Not that she needed it, seeing that her door was halfway open.

"Let me help," Dash offered, reaching for Little Blade.

"You've already been enough help, thank you very much."

"Hey, what did I do?"

She hesitated, knowing he was right. Dash didn't deserve to have her frustration taken on out him, especially when he'd basically saved her from having to ask a stranger to return her underwear. "You didn't do anything."

His eyes revealed the first sign of sympathy.

"Apparently, in my rush to get back to sing I didn't close the door all the way. It's my fault." While that was true, she did feel he was partially responsible. She refused to meet his eyes. "However, you aren't blameless."

"How's that?"

It was probably a mistake to admit this. "I wanted to show you my sexy side."

He grinned and rubbed his hand down the side of his face. "You don't need to work hard at that, Ash. I find you plenty attractive already."

Her gaze shot up and a warm feeling chased away some of the embarrassment. "You do?"

"Surprisingly so."

"Surprisingly?" How was it the man could compliment and insult her in the same breath?

"Given the fact you tried my patience to the nth degree most of the day, yes, surprisingly."

"I tried *your* patience?" She found that pretty cheeky, all things considered.

"You do. Plus, I find you distracting." He moved closer so that her back was against the wall.

"Oh?" It was hard to speak with him standing so close, especially when his gaze was focused on her lips. As he brought his face closer she held her breath in anticipation. He didn't disappoint her. Tilting his head to one side, he pressed his mouth to hers. Wrapping his hand around the back of her neck, he edged her even closer. His mouth was warm and pliable; he tasted slightly of beer, but his lengthy and exploratory kiss was what intoxicated her. A sigh rattled through him as he reluctantly dragged his mouth from hers.

Ashley kept her eyes closed as Little Blade squirmed in her arms.

"Good night, Ash."

"Night," she returned, and nearly stumbled as she stepped through the doorway. As soon as she was in the room, Ashley set Little Blade on the floor. From the mess of clothes on the floor it was clear Little Blade had had a fun time rooting through her suitcase. Unwilling to leave Dash just yet, she turned back to thank him again.

He noticed she'd peeked her head out. "I want to get an early start in the morning."

"Okay."

He frowned and glared at her as if he expected her to argue or make an unreasonable demand.

"What?" she asked.

"Nothing. It's just that I get worried when you're overly accommodating."

For him to say that was insulting. "Why would you kiss me one minute and then glare at me the next?"

"Maybe because I find myself liking you far too much."

She enjoyed the sound of that. "Is that a bad thing?"

"It could be."

"How's that?" she pressed.

"Well, for one thing, you're living in California and I'm likely to get this job in Seattle. I've done long-distance relationships before and they don't work."

At least she knew where she stood. And he'd told her before that a relationship wasn't high on his priority list. Still, she'd hoped maybe that had been starting to change. "I've got enough on my plate as it is," she added, so he'd know she wasn't interested in pursuing a relationship with him, either. "I've got to get through graduate school."

"Besides, we hardly know each other."

"One day . . . not even a full twenty-four hours," she said, although it did seem so much longer.

"Right." Even as he objected, Dash shortened the space between them.

Ashley didn't complain when he slipped his hand around her neck, easing her toward him for another intense, mindless kiss. He sighed heavily and pressed his forehead against hers. "I'll see you in the morning."

"Okay," she murmured, keeping her eyes closed as she hung on to the feelings he so easily evoked in her.

"I'll wake you at four."

"Four," she repeated, eyes shooting open. "With coffee, right?"

"With coffee."

"I don't function well without coffee." And that was putting it mildly.

"I'll see to it," he promised.

"Night," she whispered.

"Night," he repeated.

Ashley let herself into the room to find Little Blade asleep on top of her open suitcase. Scooping him up in her arms, she set him inside the carrier and closed the door.

Yawning, she changed into her pajamas, brushed her teeth, and climbed into bed, exhausted from the events of the day.

The next thing she heard was someone pounding incessantly against her door. Tossing aside the covers, Ashley stumbled toward the noise. "Coming." She checked the peephole to find Dash standing in the hallway, holding a disposable cup of coffee.

"Is it that time already?" she protested, unlatching the door.

"Morning, Sleeping Beauty."

She gratefully accepted the coffee and inhaled the scent of the brew. "I'll be ready in fifteen minutes."

His look was skeptical. "Okay. I'll have the car warmed up by the time you're dressed."

Determined not to keep Dash waiting, Ashley threw her clothes on and brought Little Blade out of the carrier and set him outside. He did his business quickly, most likely to escape the cold. The snow had stopped falling, leaving a good five or six inches on the ground.

Ashley tucked the puppy back into the carrier and met Dash in the lobby. He took Little Blade from her and she returned to her room for her suitcase. They left their key cards at the front desk and were on their way.

True to his word, Dash had the car warmed up and the windows scraped clear of frost and snow.

As soon as she was settled, Dash reiterated the importance of his arrival in Seattle that day. "The interview is this afternoon."

"I know. No unnecessary stops," she promised him.

"I'd appreciate it." He pulled out of the parking lot and they headed back to the freeway.

The car was warm and comfortable. "Did you sleep well?" he asked, after a few minutes.

"Yes. You?"

"Not so much."

"Why not?" she asked, sipping her coffee.

He didn't answer. "I had stuff on my mind."

"Are you worried about the interview?" She knew getting this job was important to him.

"No." His face darkened. "Actually, I was thinking about you and wishing things hadn't taken the turn they did last night. Don't get me wrong. I enjoyed those kisses, but now you're in my head and I can barely think of anything else."

"Really?"

"Ash, I have an important interview this afternoon and I need to focus on that. I don't need a distraction, and you're a big distraction."

"Wow."

"Don't let it go to your head."

"Sorry, too late. Might I remind you that you're the one who kissed me?"

"I know. Trust me, I know."

She could barely hide her delight. "No worries, Dash. I'll do my best to keep you focused on your interview. Is there anything I can do to help you prepare?"

"Yeah. Don't look at me like that."

"Like what?"

"Like . . . that," he muttered.

"Okay, whatever you say. Today is a clean slate."

He glanced at her. "You think you can quit being so adorable?"

Ashley thought she would melt into a puddle at his feet. "You can't say that to me and expect not to get a response. No one's ever called me adorable, at least not since I was two or three."

In an effort to help him stay focused, they rode in silence for the next hour. Ashley kept her gaze straight ahead as the miles sped by. Thankfully, the freeway was clear and the weather had improved.

It was still dark when they started over the pass into Oregon. Ashley noticed several large trucks with their taillights flashing driving on the side of the road on the steeper parts of the pass. But Dash was an excellent driver and gave the eight- and twelve-wheelers plenty of room, passing only when necessary.

As they entered Oregon, Dash looked in the rearview mirror and cursed under his breath.

"What's wrong?" she asked.

"I'm getting pulled over."

Ashley twisted around, and sure enough, the Oregon State Patrol had its lights flashing. Dash pulled over to the side of the freeway and waited for the officer to approach.

He rolled down the window and had his driver's license out. "Is there a problem?" he asked.

The officer leaned into the car and looked at Dash, Ashley, and Little Blade. "You're driving with expired license tabs."

"Impossible," Dash insisted. "This is a rental car." He leaned over Ashley, opened the glove box, and retrieved the rental agreement papers, which he handed to the patrolman.

The officer read over the sheet. "Where are you headed?" he asked.

"Seattle," Dash explained, tight-lipped.

"It looks like someone exchanged your plates. It's becoming a real problem. You'll need to report this to the rental agency when you return the car."

Dash nodded. "I'll make sure I do."

The officer returned the rental agreement and Dash's license. "Drive carefully, and remember to follow the speed limit."

"I will," Dash said.

Ashley leaned forward to smile at the officer. "Merry Christmas."

He touched the rim of his hat and smiled back. "Drive carefully, now."

Ashley waited until the officer was back in his vehicle. "I bet I know when this happened."

Dash was more concerned about getting back on the freeway and blending in with the traffic. "When?"

"Remember that kid who wanted to recite his lines in the parking lot last night?"

Dash whistled through his teeth. "His friend who joined him seemed nervous, now that I think about it."

"He looked guilty. Like he knew he was doing something wrong."

"He did," Dash agreed, frowning.

"They looked like such good kids, too." She remembered how clean cut both of them were. "Why do you think they'd do something like that?"

Dash answered with a question of his own. "Why does anyone do stuff like that?"

"Well, all I can say is what goes around comes around. That's what my dad used to tell me. I just wish I could be there to see it happen for those two kids."

Chapter Twelve

Agent Jordan Wilkes ended his phone conversation and turned to Agent Buckley, who was driving ten miles above the speed limit. Wilkes had spent a restless night mostly without sleep, reviewing what information they had with the hope that they were on the right track with Ashley Davison. Again and again his mind turned over the relationship between the woman and the former army intelligence officer and their possible connection.

Although they had little to go on, Wilkes continued to travel north. His gut told him they were close to capturing Davison and making an arrest. As he neared the end of his career, capturing Ashley Davison would cap his long years of service.

His phone beeped. He answered, listened, and then triumphantly told Agent Buckley, "We got a hit." He knew he was close. He'd felt it, and after the last two years of hitting one dead end after another, he could taste victory.

"Where?" Buckley asked.

"About twenty miles ahead. I'll contact the local authorities and get a chopper to keep track of the vehicle."

Buckley waited until Wilkes had made the arrangements, which involved three different government agencies. "I won't make the mistake of underestimating Ashley Davison again," the older, more experienced agent insisted. "This time I'm calling in every agency available for reinforcements. We have her now and I'm going to trap her in so tight there's no possible way she'll escape."

"You ordered a helicopter?"

"Yes. It's important we take every precaution. The woman and the situation are dangerous. She's got a hostage, and she'll use whatever means is available to escape capture. God only knows what she wants from Dash Sutherland and how much she's already been able to get out of him. It would be a shame for him to escape injury in Afghanistan only to be killed by a homegrown American terrorist."

"A shame for sure," Agent Buckley agreed.

His cell rang again and he answered. "Wilkes."

The conversation was brief, and he noticed that the other agent was keenly interested. "I told you Davison was clever," he said once he'd disconnected. "I swear the woman has a sixth sense. The 'copter has the car in sight. She's left the freeway and is driving side roads. It's like she can smell us closing in on her." He checked his weapon. While he didn't want to use it, if the situation called for gunfire, Wilkes wouldn't hesitate.

"The local authorities have been told to stay back. We don't want to give Davison any indication that she's been detected and is being followed."

"What about the chopper?"

Wilkes knew what his subordinate was asking. "The bird is keeping a safe distance from the vehicle so as not to be detected." His fellow team members had been trained in avoiding discovery. He trusted them to handle this situation with the same expertise they had in other operations. Ashley Davison didn't know it yet, but she was headed straight for prison. By the time she was released, if ever, Wilkes would be enjoying his retirement on a Hawaiian isle.

"Travis, do you hear that noise?" Justin asked, as they headed toward Bailey's house, taking the slow, meandering river road.

"What noise?" Travis asked, messing with the radio.

"It sounds like a helicopter."

"So?"

"So," his friend said, gazing out the passenger window, "it seems to be following us."

Travis shook his head. Justin had a creative imagination. "You're nuts. Why would a helicopter follow us? It isn't like we're escaped felons. Trading license plates can't be anything more than a misdemeanor, if that. Even if we are caught, the courts would probably only give us community service or probation. We're both honor students, right?"

"I'm not," Justin corrected. "Mrs. Lael gave me a C-minus in English."

"No kidding?" The fact was Travis's grades had fallen short last semester as well. "Okay, we used to be honor students."

"Right." Justin rolled down his window and stuck his head out, hoping to get a better view of the chopper.

"See anything?"

"Yeah, the 'copter is holding back, but it's still keeping us in sight. It's black."

"Black? Is that supposed to mean something?" Travis was amused. Justin had been reading too many spy novels. "You're getting paranoid."

"Maybe ... maybe not. Remember that movie we watched with Mel Gibson on Netflix a while back, the one where he had all these escape routes set up in his apartment? Everyone thought he was nuts, but in the end the government came for him and he managed to break free because he'd taken all those precautions. My dad doesn't trust the government and neither do I. Dad and his buddies talk about it all the time."

"Do you seriously think there are men in black jackets who descend from helicopters, dude?"

"Think?" Justin repeated. "I don't need to think—there's one following us right this minute."

"Do you see anyone dressed in black?"

Justin was clearly obsessed. "No," he admitted reluctantly.

"Could be aliens," Travis teased, and watched as Justin's face reddened.

Justin stuck his cell out the window and took a photo. "You think I've gone wacko, don't you?"

"Hey, man, I was just needling you."

"Well, don't," he muttered, and then shouted, "Hurry, take the next right."

"Why?"

"I want to see what that chopper does."

Travis was willing to humor his friend, but as far as he could tell this conspiracy theory was ridiculous. No one was following them. It had to be Justin's overactive imagination.

"Oh man." His friend's voice lowered and actually trembled.

"What?"

"There's about six cars all following us. They look like unmarked police cars."

Travis nearly laughed out loud. Justin was losing it. "How do you know they're police cars?"

"I'm telling you, they're police or government vehicles. Who else drives black Suburbans? It's like a funeral procession."

Justin made it sound as if it was their funeral. "And you think they're after us?"

"I know they are. Speed up, dude."

In an effort to appease his friend, Travis hit fifty-five in a thirty-five-mile-per-hour zone. Checking his rearview mirror, he momentarily caught sight of the six cars as he took a turn in the road. They looked like a long black snake following him along the river road, twisting and turning. Travis wasn't caught up in the conspiracy craziness the way Justin was, but he was beginning to get worried.

"The chopper's closing in," Justin shouted, his voice edged in panic.

Travis looked up and saw two men on each side of the chopper, sitting in open doors. His own heart started to pound. *They were all dressed in black*. He gasped when he saw ropes descend. His fifty-five-mile-an-hour speed quickly zoomed to sixty and then seventy as the long row of cars quickly narrowed the distance between them, racing at a breakneck pace behind them.

"What should I do?" Travis shouted. It appeared Justin wasn't as nutso as he'd thought.

Justin seemed paralyzed with fear and Travis wasn't far behind. This was crazy. He looked over to see his friend had whipped out his cell and was frantically pushing numbers.

"Who are you texting?"

"My dad. I sent him the photo of the chopper . . . he'll know what to do."

Travis had his foot all the way to the floor. At the next curve along the twisting road he nearly lost control. It felt as if his car had gone up on two wheels before righting itself. No matter how fast he went, the string of black cars continued to get closer. Within minutes, they were directly behind him.

From out of nowhere, a bullhorn blast came that nearly burst Travis's eardrums.

"This is the FBI. Pull over."

"The FBI. Should I do it?" Travis asked in a panic.

"If you do, our parents will never see us again."

"We might not have any choice," Travis said, his words thick with terror. The chopper had lowered to the point that it hung directly over their moving car.

"If I don't show," Travis cried, "Bailey will kill me."

"Then get us out of this."

"I'm trying."

But soon they were given no option. The road up ahead was blocked and the FBI was hot on their tail.

Shaking with fear, Travis eased to a halt.

"Put your hands up where I can see them," the voice from the bullhorn instructed them.

Travis and Justin thrust their arms out the open window and followed instructions.

"Step out of the vehicle, hands where I can see them."

They opened the doors and climbed out of the car. Travis couldn't be sure, but he thought he heard one of the men swear, followed by a shocked voice: "It's two kids."

Within seconds they were surrounded by men with their weapons drawn. Following the shouted orders, they got down on their knees with their hands locked behind their heads.

"Check for weapons."

One of the agents, who seemed to be the one in charge, approached them. "What did I tell you, Buckley?" he muttered. "Davison is a master of escape. She must have traded license plates with this car. Same year, same model. The woman has eluded us once again."

The woman, Travis thought. The man must be talking about the woman he spoke to in the Walmart parking lot.

"She traded plates?" the other agent asked.

"Looks like she set us up."

Travis and Justin shared a look. Neither one was about to explain that the woman wasn't responsible.

"It's back to square one."

"Not yet it isn't," the first agent who spoke insisted. "Not by a long shot. I'm not giving up until Davison is behind bars where she belongs."

Chapter Thirteen

Dash and Ashley stopped for gas in Ashland, Oregon. When she was in her early teens Ashley's parents had taken her and her brother to a Shakespeare festival in Ashland. Ashley had never forgotten the experience and had fond memories of the town.

While Dash dealt with filling up the car, Ashley took Little Blade for a short walk and gave him some water. The weather wasn't as cold and the threat of snow had passed. Her hope was that it would be smooth driving from this point forward.

Once back in the car, Dash eased into the freeway traffic.

"Do you think you'll like living in Seattle?" she asked. He'd already mentioned that he didn't know anyone in town, having been born and raised in Texas.

"Don't see why I wouldn't, but don't get ahead of yourself. I don't have the job yet."

"You'll get it." She was confident. He'd felt equally assured earlier, but as they drew closer to their destination, doubts seemed to be forming. He seemed to have a lot of nervous energy and had grown less talkative. Ashley suspected his mind was on the upcoming interview.

"I appreciate the positive thinking."

"You've got the training and the background," she said, in an effort to boost his confidence. "From what you've told me, you're a perfect fit. The company must need you badly to ask you to come for an interview this close to the holidays."

"That was my thought, too," he added, and he seemed to relax.

"Seattle is a great city," she continued. "There's so much to do living in the Pacific Northwest." She went on to mention the hiking trails, the skiing opportunities, and boating and annual festivals, all of which she enjoyed.

"Will you move back here once you have your degree?" Dash asked, once she'd finished talking.

His question raised one of her own: Did he hope she would live in Seattle? Being close to family was what she wanted, but there were other factors to consider. "I hope to, but it depends on where I can find a job."

"I know the feeling," he said, and then added, his voice lowering to a sexy murmur, "I hope you do."

Ashley's heart raced. "You do?"

"Your roots are in the area. It's apparent you and your mother are close and rely on each other."

Ashley examined the square-cut edges of her fingernails. "So would you like it if I lived in Seattle?"

He momentarily looked away from the road. "Yeah, I'd like it a lot."

For just a second Ashley couldn't breathe. She'd met Dash a little less than twenty-four hours ago and she felt closer to him in that short amount of time than she had to any man she'd dated in a long time. Already her mind was thinking of ways for them to stay in touch after the holidays. She didn't want to be presumptuous, and yet she felt this connection with him—this very strong connection. She knew he felt it, too.

Unexpectedly, Dash muttered a curse under his breath.

"What now?" she asked, checking behind her to be sure there wasn't another patrol car pulling them over.

"The engine light just came on," he explained.

The car was practically new. At one point Dash had mentioned it had less than twenty-five thousand miles on it. "What does it say?"

"Check engine," he clarified.

"Not very detailed, is it?"

"Not very timely, either. I'll pull into one of the truck stops and find out where there's a dealership or a good mechanic. I don't want to take a chance of breaking down on the freeway. We could get stuck for hours."

Ashley agreed it would be best to deal with the problem now rather than wait for something to go wrong. Too much was at stake.

They drove with the engine light blinking until they reached Grants Pass. Dash pulled into a truck stop and had her stay in the car while he found out what he could. He wasn't gone more than a few minutes.

"There's a reliable mechanic just a mile north of here. I got the directions."

"Do you think we should contact the rental car people?"

"No. They might want us to trade vehicles, and who knows how long that will take. All I want to do is find out what's wrong and see if the car will get us to Seattle without a problem."

That sounded like a good idea. Ashley understood his concern. A great deal was riding on this interview, and Dash didn't want to take a chance of anything delaying them any more than it already had.

Dash found the repair shop without a problem and

pulled up front. He climbed out of the car. By this point, Ashley was ready to stretch her legs.

A man in gray striped overalls stepped out of the garage, a pink rag tucked into his back pocket. He wore a cap with his hair sticking out from beneath it and had a beard.

"What can I do for you folks?" he asked. He had to be in his midfifties and rubbed his oil-smudged hands on the pink rag.

Dash explained the problem.

"Name's Stan. Folks around these parts call me Stan the Man."

"Any particular reason?" Ashley asked, assuming it was because he was the man everyone came to when they had car troubles. She was hoping for reassurance that he would know exactly what needed to be done and would be able to fix it in a hurry and send them happily on their way.

Dash pulled the lever to release the hood.

"Funny you should ask," Stan said, edging up the bill of his hat. "You see, ten years ago I was kidnapped by aliens."

Dash nearly hit his head on the hood of the car, he jerked up so fast. "What'd you say?"

"I know, I know, most folks think I'm off my rocker, but the fact is I've been inside an alien spaceship."

"I see," Ashley whispered, sorry now that she'd asked.

"A good bit of what I know about machines and how

they run came from my time with my alien friends. People come to me from all over the state because they know I'll fix whatever's wrong with their cars."

"So you're something of an engine whisperer?" Ashley asked.

Dash shot her a look that suggested she not get any more involved in the conversation than necessary.

"Seeing that you're good with engines, can you tell me what the problem is here?"

"Sure thing." Stan the Man leaned over the hood. "Fell in love with a hot alien chick," he stated matter-of-factly. "She was a beaut. Actually, she kinda reminds me of you," he said, turning his head to smile at Ashley. "Only she was seven feet tall. Maybe seven-one, now that I think about it."

"Oh." Ashley took a step back.

"She taught me a lot about the joy of alien sex. They do things in ways you and I have never even dreamed of."

This was definitely a subject Ashley wanted to avoid. "How nice."

"She had my baby, told me she'd name him after me. Never did find out if she had a boy or a girl. I was sort of hoping for a son. Never had a son. Truth is, I never married. Women around these parts are too picky."

"About the car," Dash said, in a blatant effort to get Stan to focus on the problem at hand.

"I'm getting to it. Don't rush me. These are delicate machines and it has to talk to me first."

"You communicate with engines?" Ashley supposed it made sense. If he could father an alien child, then getting a car engine to talk to him must be as easy as pie.

"Of course cars talk," Stan the Man returned, as if that was one of the dumbest questions he'd ever heard. "Most everyone sees cars as inanimate objects, but that isn't so. That's another thing my alien friends taught me." That said, Stan the Man leaned over the engine a second time. He twisted his head so his ear was close and then held up his hand as if asking for quiet. A couple times he nodded as if agreeing to what the engine had to tell him.

Dash caught Ashley's look and gestured helplessly with his hands. Ashley squelched a laugh. How was it that they met up with these characters? This was nuts and at the same time a lot of fun, whether Dash wanted to admit it or not. She liked Stan the Man. Okay, he was a bit odd, but he wasn't scary. In fact, she found him cute in an odd sort of way.

After a couple of moments, Stan the Man straightened and then scratched his forehead, leaving a smear of oil across his brow.

"What did the engine say?" Dash asked, apparently deciding to play along with the mechanic's unconventional methods.

"She's not saying much."

"Tight-lipped women can be a real headache," Dash muttered. "Then again, the fact they aren't speaking can be a blessing."

Ashley narrowed a look at him, scalding him with her eyes. Then she turned to the mechanic. "The car's a female?" she asked, and for some unexplainable reason that pleased her.

"Most definitely," Stan the Man assured her. "By the way, she's glad you decided to take the puppy. Not sure what that meant, but I figured you'd know."

Ashley's eyebrows shot up. Now, that was impressive.

"I thought you said she wasn't saying much," Dash reminded him.

"Well, she's not, at least not about what seems to be troubling her, but she has lots to say about other stuff."

"Like what?" Ashley couldn't help being curious.

"The puppy, for one. She seems to have strong opinions about the two of you."

"Could we stick with what needs to be fixed so we can get back on the road?" Dash requested, clearly losing patience.

"I'm trying."

"Maybe if we looked in the owner's manual," Ashley suggested, in a effort to be helpful. She slipped back into the front seat and opened the glove compartment.

Stan the Man shook his head. "You can read all you want, but that's not going to help."

Dash muttered something unintelligible and then walked away in an apparent effort to keep his cool. He glanced at his watch and Ashley knew he was calculating the travel time. Ashley wasn't concerned. Even if they were stuck for another hour he would still have plenty of time to make the interview.

"You never did explain why you're called Stan the Man," Ashley said, and immediately wished she hadn't at the wide-eyed look that came from Dash. Clearly, he wanted to get back on the road, and her delaying with a bunch of nonessential questions wasn't helping.

In Dash's mind, he must think they were dealing with someone who belonged in the loony bin. Ashley wasn't so sure. She saw the loving way Stan the Man ran his hands over the engine, twisting cables and checking this and that, much of which remained a mystery to her.

"Ah yes. I tend to get sidetracked when I tell people about my alien wife." He smiled and pulled the rag from his hip pocket and wiped his hands. "She was a looker. Friends gave me the name. They said that for me to seduce an alien I must be some kind of man. I should have corrected them. She seduced me, but I was willing. That woman was hot."

Dash paced the area in front of the car.

"Start her up," Stan instructed. "And see if that engine light flashes back on."

Eagerly, Dash climbed into the driver's seat and turned the key. The engine roared to life, and Dash focused his attention on the dashboard. After a couple of seconds, his face broke into a smile and he gave Stan a thumbs-up.

"It looks like we're good, then." Stan patted the engine as if it were a well-behaved child.

"What did you do?" Dash wanted to know, as he climbed out of the car and left the engine running.

Ashley was curious herself. She hadn't seen Stan do anything more than lower his head and supposedly listen to the car talk to him before twisting a couple of cables.

"She just needed to know she's respected. Rental cars can be finicky, seeing that they have someone new behind the wheel every few days. She's had to deal with quite a lot since the factory released her. She doesn't feel she's appreciated." He lowered the hood and gave her a gentle pat.

Dash was about to blurt out something, but Ashley's hand on his arm stopped him.

"How much do I owe you?" he asked, reaching for his wallet in his hip pocket.

Stan the Man held up both hands. "It's on the house."

"No, I insist." Dash took out two large bills and stuffed them in the pocket of Stan's coveralls.

"Not necessary, but I appreciate it," Stan the Man said.

"You ready to go?" Dash asked, looking at Ashley.

"Oh sure." On impulse, she hugged Stan. He was a character, and while it seemed unlikely that he had actually fathered an alien baby or could convince cars to give up their secrets, he was a likable guy.

They climbed into the car, but before Dash could close the door, Stan the Man stopped him. "You and your woman have a merry Christmas."

"Thanks," Ashley said, beaming him a smile.

Dash frowned. "She's not my woman."

Stan grinned, revealing a row of uneven, yellowing teeth. "Not yet, but something tells me she will be soon enough."

"Something tells you?" Dash repeated. "You mean like that block of steel engine?"

Stan widened his eyes. "You need to be more sensitive, young man. That car's got feelings."

"Oh sorry," Dash returned, and gently patted the steering wheel as if petting Little Blade.

Stan the Man stepped back as Dash backed out of the space in front of the garage.

"Was that not the weirdest guy you've ever met?" he asked, shaking his head as if he continued to find the entire encounter nothing short of bizarre.

"He was certainly entertaining."

"He's off his rocker."

"You're just jealous," Ashley teased. "I saw that gleam

in your eyes. You want one of those hot alien chicks for yourself."

Dash snorted, mocking her. "No thanks. I've got all I can handle with you."

With her? That was by far the most romantic thing he'd ever said to her.

Chapter Fourteen

Back on I-5, Dash glanced over at Ashley; actually, she'd noticed that he had a hard time keeping his eyes on the road. He seemed to be glancing at her more and more frequently. "What's that secret little smile about?" he asked.

"I'm not smiling." Just to be on the safe side, she tossed him a dour look.

"Now you're not, but you were a few seconds ago."

"I can smile if I want," she insisted.

Little Blade whined from the backseat.

Motioning toward the backseat, he said, "See, even the dog agrees."

"Men," she clucked, shaking her head. "You all stick together. Why should it bother you when I smile? One would think you'd be happy that I'm happy."

"It wasn't that you were smiling, it was the way you were doing it . . . like you had this deep, dark secret and were intent on keeping it from me."

"I can assure you I don't have any nefarious secrets. I'm not a spy or an alien about to take you to my spaceship."

He chuckled, apparently finding her amusing. "I should be so lucky."

"Hey, you were singing a different tune just a few minutes ago."

He seemed more relaxed now. "So you don't want to explain that smile?" Dash questioned.

"All right, if you must know, I was thinking that maybe we should thank this car for getting us where we need to go. We'll be in Seattle in plenty of time for you to make your interview."

"Let's hope."

At the rate they were currently traveling, it wouldn't be a problem. "Stan the Man was right. Being owned by a rental agency must be trying on a car. New drivers every other day, uncaring folks who drive recklessly and leave their empty fast-food bags scattered about. I bet she sees her share of spills, too."

"Don't be ridiculous," he chided. "Cars don't have feelings, no matter what Stan claims. And they don't talk, either."

Ashley could see that he was more amused than annoyed, although he did his best to pretend otherwise. She might have been fooled if she hadn't noticed the edges of his mouth twitching to hold back a smile.

"Will you call me after the interview?" she asked, before she remembered that he no longer had a phone.

"Why?"

"So I can hear how it went. I know you want this job, and I'll be anxious to hear how everything goes."

"I would if I had a phone."

"I know. I realized that right after I asked. Don't you feel naked without it? I know I would, and mine, for now anyway, is just a flip phone."

"Did you ask Santa for a smartphone?"

"Oh yes, top of my list. I've got a laptop . . ."

"With you?"

"No. If I brought it I knew I'd be constantly studying and fussing with email. This time away is a gift for both Mom and me, and I didn't want to spoil it by getting caught up in classwork."

"That's thoughtful."

She grinned. "I am capable of being a caring, compassionate woman, Dash. Don't sound so surprised."

He snorted. "I figured that much when you insisted on rescuing Little Blade."

They continued driving and then curiosity got the better of her. "You want to tell me about the girl who dumped you?" she asked, as conversationally as she could manage.

"What? Who told you that?" He took his eyes off the road long enough to question her.

"You. Don't you remember? You were fairly adamant that long-distance relationships don't work. I have to assume this was someone you were involved with while you were in Afghanistan."

"I don't want to go there."

She was curious, but decided to let it drop. "No problem, but it's a shame."

"What is? That I don't want to get involved with you?"

She hesitated and then figured she had nothing to lose. "It's more than that. I get the feeling you don't want to get involved . . . period. It isn't only me."

He barked a laugh that didn't hold any amusement. "Thank you, Dr. Phil."

"You're welcome."

He turned her words back on her. "I seem to recall you telling me you weren't willing to get involved, either. Something about concentrating on your studies and not having time, blah, blah, blah."

"I lied."

"You lied? You're admitting you lied?"

"I felt I had to," she confessed. "I mean, here you were, so eager to discount the kiss we'd shared. So what was I supposed to say? Your kiss was . . . wow. It was great, and then this morning you had to set matters straight by letting me know you didn't want any distractions. Apparently, the kisses weren't the same for you as they were for me, and so yes, I lied."

Dash paused and then admitted in a low voice, "Okay, you're right. I said I didn't want to think about it, but I have nearly every minute since."

"In other words, you lied, too." Her smile was wide enough to cause her mouth to ache.

"I didn't want to mislead you."

That made no sense. "You didn't want to mislead me, so you misled me?" She shook her head in an effort to make sense of that. "You're confusing me."

"I'm confused, too. This thing with us, if you can even call it a thing, came out of nowhere. When we met up at the airport I was convinced you were going to be a royal pain."

"Me? Okay, to be fair, I wasn't high on you, either."

"I didn't expect to like you or to feel this . . . connection, for lack of a better word. It's like I got hit between the eyes, and it couldn't happen at a worse time."

Ashley knew how he felt.

"I want this job, Ash, and this is the worst time possible for me to be distracted."

"And I'm a distraction." She knew it was true. He should be mentally preparing himself for this interview.

"Yes. If I get this job, which I want and need, it'll basically put me in the same situation as before, and I don't do long-distance relationships."

"And if you don't get it . . ."

"If I don't get the job, I've got to start over with no guarantees that I'll continue to live in the Bay Area. I'd like to see you again . . ."

"I'd like to see you, too. Instead of fretting about this now, why don't we wait until after the interview?"

He agreed, and reaching over, he grasped her hand, squeezing her fingers. It was hard to describe the emotions Ashley felt at his touch. Neither of them had been expecting this. The timing was all wrong for him and for her. Still, she couldn't imagine not seeing Dash after this trip, and she hoped he felt the same.

"Can we talk about something else now?" he asked.

"Sure. Looks pretty out there."

He relaxed. "Actually, it's overcast, and I heard there's a chance of snow around the Portland area."

"Kids will love that. You like kids, don't you?"

He shrugged. "As long as they're someone else's."

"You don't want children?" she asked, and then realized she might be broaching a taboo subject. Quickly, she held up both hands and, pretending to be horrified, added, "Don't answer that."

"Why not?"

"I was trying to not talk about anything personal, you know, to distract you."

"Some questions I don't mind answering. As for you wanting to know about me and having kids, the answer is yes, I'd like a couple of kids someday."

"Just not in the foreseeable future."

"Right. Satisfied?"

"Yes." They were riding in a companionable silence when Ashley noticed she was hungry. In fact, she was famished. The only thing she'd had to eat or drink all day was the cup of coffee Dash had brought her early that morning.

"Can we stop for food? I'm starving." It all became clear to her then. "That explains it," she said righteously.

"Explains what?"

"Why you're . . . preoccupied." She didn't want to say he was cranky, because he wasn't. "You get that way when you're hungry. Remember yesterday when I fed you my protein bar?"

"I am not testy."

"True, but you'll do better on the interview if you've eaten properly."

"The interview isn't until later."

"I know that," she countered. "Besides, Little Blade needs a potty break." She did as well, but she wasn't about to make a point of it. There were certain personal subjects she would prefer to avoid.

"Okay, fine. But let's make it fast food. I want to get into Seattle as quickly as I can."

"Whatever you want."

He frowned. "I worry when you get overly accommodating. It's like when a woman says, 'Correct me if I'm wrong . . .' Trust me, most men know never to make that mistake. It's a trap."

Ashley was not amused. "You have a low opinion of women."

He grinned. "As a matter of fact, I don't. I happen to like you—for the most part, anyway."

"You did it again."

"Did what?"

"You criticize me in what should be a compliment."

Dash frowned.

"What's that saying . . . damning me with faint praise? Sounds like something Shakespeare wrote, but I don't think he did."

"How was I criticizing you?" He seemed genuinely curious.

"You mean you honestly don't know? You just said that for the *most part* you liked me, which implies there are certain parts of me you find irritating."

"You mean to say you don't find me irritating at times?"

"More so every minute," she said with a snicker.

"Now look who's cranky. There's an exit coming up. McDonald's, Burger King, KFC. The choice is yours."

"Any of those is fine."

"Oh no, I'm not falling for that. The minute I pick one, you'll want the other."

"That is so not true."

"All right, Burger King."

She smiled as if the sun set and rose on his choice. "Perfect."

Dash took the exit and followed the signs leading to a long row of fast-food establishments. Thankfully, they'd already made their decision, because there were a dozen others just as close.

The Burger King was on the right-hand side, and Dash was able to turn in to a long line of cars queuing up for the drive-through. Without her even asking, Dash ordered a hamburger patty for Little Blade.

"That was thoughtful." He'd surprised and impressed her.

"I can be thoughtful."

"I know." When it came their turn, Dash insisted on paying. They parked in the lot and Dash turned off the engine. "We can eat inside if you want."

"No, it's fine." She didn't want to leave Little Blade in the car alone. Between bites of her burger, she tore off small bits of meat to feed to the puppy, who gobbled it up fast and licked her fingers, seeking more.

After a restroom break, Dash collected their garbage. He got out of the car and emptied their wrappers into the trash can.

"I think I'm losing it," he said when he returned.

"How so?" She wasn't clear on what he meant.

"I didn't want to hurt the car's feelings, so I got rid of the trash instead of leaving it in the car."

Ashley smiled.

In response, he reached for her by the shoulders, pulling her toward him, and gave her an open-mouthed kiss that left her dizzy and warm and utterly stunned. And utterly happy.

Chapter Fifteen

The frustration was killing Agent Jordan Wilkes. He was close to making the biggest capture of his career and once again had been thwarted by one of the cleverest criminal masterminds he'd encountered in his thirty-year time with the bureau. It was no wonder Ashley Davison had eluded the law these last two years. Capturing her would be the pinnacle of his career with the FBI.

"What now?" Agent Buckley asked.

"We wait," Wilkes told the younger agent. Patience was a key virtue when it came to being an agent, and it often paid big dividends. Agent Buckley would learn that lesson soon enough, if he remained in the agency.

"How long should we wait?"

"However long it takes." Crime knew no holiday. Wilkes couldn't remember the last Christmas he'd spent with his wife and family. But if sacrificing Christmas gave him the opportunity to aprehend Ashley Davison, then it would be worth it. He wanted this woman's capture on his record, and he wanted it badly.

As he knew it would, his cell buzzed. "Wilkes," he answered, doing his best to hide his eagerness to hear the latest update.

The disembodied voice came fast and furious over the line: "An Oregon state patrolman pulled them over."

"Where?"

"Outside of Ashland."

"Tell him to keep them in custody until we get there. Call in backup; I don't want to take a chance of letting Davison slip through our fingers again."

After a slight pause, the agent on the other end of the line continued: "He let them go."

"What? How in the hell did that happen?"

"This was before we realized they'd switched license plates. It was the same year and model in the bulletin. That was what caught his attention, but the plates were different."

"Why'd he pull them over?" The officer must have had a reason. The bulletin that had gone out to law enforcement agencies said to look for a woman holding a man hostage.

"He pulled them over for expired tabs."

So Davison wasn't as clever as she thought. If she was going to exchange license plates, she should have noticed the one she switched had outdated tabs. This was just the break Wilkes was looking for. "I want to interview the officer."

"I have him right here."

A short pause followed. "This is Officer Jamison."

"Yes, Officer, thank you." Wilkes looked toward his partner and nodded, indicating they weren't about to give up yet. His gut had told him Davison was close.

"I stopped the vehicle at Milepost 431 for expired tabs."

"You saw the photo of Dashiell Sutherland and identified him?"

"I did," the state patrolman verified. "I wasn't able to positively identify the woman from the photo."

That was understandable, seeing how clever Davison had been about hiding her identity. The woman was a tease. She got her jollies from thwarting law enforcement. But her time was running out . . . sands through an hourglass.

"Was the woman driving?" Wilkes asked.

"No, the man was."

It made sense that she'd force Sutherland to take the wheel. "What kind of vibe did you get from him?"

"Vibe?"

"Did he show signs of stress? Did he appear overly nervous?" Wilkes asked, hoping to get something that would help in Davison's ultimate capture.

"Not really," the patrolman answered. "All drivers show signs of stress when pulled over."

"Did you detect anything suspicious or out of the ordinary?" he asked next.

"No . . ."

"What is it, man?" Wilkes demanded, sensing the patrol officer wanted to tell him something more.

"There was a dog. A puppy. He was asleep in the backseat."

"We know about the dog."

Jamison hesitated. "There was something else . . . I don't know if it's relevant, but . . ."

"Yes," Wilkes coaxed.

"The woman was overly friendly with me."

"Overly friendly?"

"Yes, she leaned forward, offered me a big smile, and wished me a merry Christmas."

Wilkes could picture the scene in his mind. Ashley Davison had made a narrow escape. Not for the first time, she'd managed to outsmart law enforcement, and naturally she was relieved. She hadn't been flirting—that wasn't her style—she was simply happy, riding high on her success.

She'd made a mistake, though. A big one. And she assumed she'd gotten off scot-free. She didn't know it yet, but that was about to change.

"Anything else you can tell us?"

"Yes," Officer Jamison continued. "Later I got a call near Grants Pass. I believe I saw the car I'd stopped earlier take the first exit. There are a number of gas stations in the area, so I suspect they were looking to fill their tank."

More good news. "Thank you, Officer. You've been a big help."

"Glad to be of assistance," he said, and disconnected the line. The state patrolman didn't know how fortunate he was. If he'd caught on that there was something amiss, Wilkes was fairly certain the woman would have done whatever necessary to keep him from reporting her whereabouts. Instead, Jamison would head home to his family. If luck was with Wilkes, he, too, might be able to join his own family for Christmas this year. All he had to do was apprehend Ashley Davison.

"Start the car," Wilkes instructed his partner. "We've got the lead we've been waiting for." He felt the adrenaline rush. He was familiar enough with the feeling that told him he was close to capturing his prize. It wouldn't be long now. Not long at all.

———

Wilkes and Buckley hit pay dirt at the third gas station. It was a big truck stop and sold only diesel. He'd almost by-passed it, but he was determined to leave no stone unturned. It was there that he found what he needed to know.

"Yeah." The young woman behind the counter wore her dirty-blond hair in a ponytail. She looked at the photo again and said, "That's him, all right. He was here maybe an hour ago. Maybe it was thirty minutes. I lose track of time. He wasn't looking to fill up his car. Couldn't have helped him if he was, but he already seemed to know that."

A trucker stepped up to the counter, and without break-ing eye contact with Wilkes, Ponytail handed over the key attached to a large flat board that read SHOWER ROOM.

"He was looking for the name of a good mechanic," she continued. "I told him about Stan the Man. He's a bit of an odd duck, but he's good with cars. He knows his busi-ness."

"Stan the Man. That's the name of his business?"

"Nope, that's his name. Never heard him called any-thing else. Don't know his last name."

Wilkes decided to let that pass. "Did the man in the photograph mention what kind of car trouble he was hav-ing?"

The young woman shook her head. "No, can't say that he did. His best chance of getting back on the road in a hurry, though, was with Stan the Man—"

"He was in a hurry?" he asked, interrupting her.

"Yes, big-time. I think he said something about an appointment in Seattle."

"Today?" His heart started to race. A sense of urgency filled him. Whatever was going down must be taking place soon. Sooner than he'd anticipated. This news didn't bode well.

"I can't say when or why he needed to get to Seattle." She shrugged, and looked like she regretted not being able to help him more.

"Okay, let's get back to the mechanic you recommended."

"Stan the Man's the best we have, probably the best in the entire county. He knows cars better than anyone."

"Anything else you can tell us?"

"Not that I remember."

Agent Buckley handed her a card. "If you think of anything, just call this number."

"I will," she said, reading the card. She glanced up and smiled. "I've never talked to anyone in the FBI before."

"We need to get back on the road," Wilkes said, and grabbed the photo off the counter.

"You've been a big help," Agent Buckley told Ponytail.

Wilkes waited until they were back in the black Suburban before he spoke. "Whatever is going down is happening soon."

"I don't understand why Sutherland didn't say something to the clerk. Davison wasn't around."

"That we know of," Wilkes muttered. Agent Buckley
wasn't as familiar with Davison as he was. "The woman
could easily have had something on Sutherland that made it
impossible for him to talk."

"If luck is with us, he'll still be at the repair shop."

Wilkes hoped that was the case; they'd find out soon
enough.

"Should we call for backup?" Agent Buckley asked.

Thinking of the fiasco that had so recently taken place,
Wilkes decided to wait. "We'll do surveillance first and then
make that decision."

They arrived at the address and circled the block. The
garage bay doors were open and it was apparent they were
too late to apprehend Davison and release her hostage.

As soon as they parked in front of the business, the tall,
thin man in overalls walked out to greet them. He wore a
big smile.

"I've been waiting for you boys for fifteen years," he
said, grinning for all he was worth as he wiped his hands
clean on a pink rag.

Wilkes and Buckley exchanged glances.

"All I can say is that it took you long enough. I must have
written and emailed you a hundred times and never got a
response. What did it this time?"

"You're Stan."

"Stan the Man," he corrected. "Folks around here gave me the name because of my alien wife."

"What country is she from?"

"Not a country, man. She's from a different planet."

"You have a wife from outer space?" Buckley asked incredulously.

Ah hell. Wilkes was afraid this was going to be a waste of precious time. This mechanic was a candidate for a padded cell.

"Yup, she's from a planet mankind has yet to discover. I hated to leave her pregnant and all. Been waiting all these years to get back to her."

"We aren't here about space travel," Wilkes informed him, doing what he could to get the information he needed. He should have taken note when the dirty-blond told him Stan the Man was a bit of an odd duck. That was putting it mildly.

"You aren't here about me and my alien wife?" Stan the Man didn't bother to hide his disappointment.

"We need to know if you've seen this man in the last few hours." Wilkes held up the photograph of Dash Sutherland.

The mechanic studied the photo and slowly a smile slid into place. He looked up and held Wilkes's gaze for a long moment. "Tell you what. You scratch my back and I'll scratch yours."

"I beg your pardon?"

By this time Stan looked almost gleeful. "You heard me. You need my help and I need yours."

Wilkes stiffened. "What do you want?"

"It'll be no skin off your nose, so don't go all pissy on me. I want to go up in one of those rockets the government is always shooting off down there in Florida. I want to find my woman and lay claim to my child."

Wilkes had heard a great deal in his years with the FBI, but this was by far the most unusual request of his career.

"I tried all the normal channels to get back to my lover, but my congressman considered me a nutcase and our senator hasn't bothered to answer a single one of my requests. I'm tired of playing nice. If you boys can't help me, then I'm done answering your questions. We're finished here." He looked expectantly from one to the other.

For one of the first times in his career, Wilkes was speechless.

"I know you have ways of making me talk, but I'm telling you right now that unless you're willing to play ball, my lips are sealed."

It was Buckley who took the lead. "We might be able to arrange something."

Stan's face widened with a satisfied grin. "I thought you boys would see the light. Oh, and by the way, your car needs an oil change."

Wilkes glanced over his shoulder to make sure the Suburban wasn't leaking oil. "How do you know that?"

"He told me," Stan the Man explained. "For the most part, he's proud to be part of the support staff for the FBI, but you need to see that he's properly fed and given what he needs."

Chapter Sixteen

"Do you have dreams?" Ashley asked Dash, curiosity getting the better of her. They were well into Oregon now and she was relaxed and feeling particularly close to Dash. No matter how much he wanted to concentrate on the upcoming interview, he couldn't ignore the attraction between them. Maybe it was the holiday season or the fact that they'd been in close proximity to each other for the last two days. No matter what brought this about, she wasn't complaining. The pressure of work and school had vanished and she was more relaxed than she had been in months. Her head and her heart felt wide open.

While it was true they'd just met, they'd spent more time

together in the last day and a half than she had with Jackson, a man she'd been dating on again/off again for several months—well, until recently.

"Everyone dreams," Dash said, glancing her way and smiling. "Personally, I don't remember mine."

"Not nighttime dreams," she chided, and resisted rolling her eyes. He was being deliberately obtuse, which she discovered was something he enjoyed. "Dreams, you know, about your future."

"Oh, those kind of dreams. Yeah, I suppose," he said without elaborating. "What about you?"

She sighed and leaned her head against the back of the seat. Little Blade had gotten restless after their lunch stop and she'd brought him into the front seat with her. He was sprawled across her lap and she absently petted him. The puppy was content now and she was growing sleepy.

"My immediate dreams are to finish my graduate degree and find work. I'd like to be close to Mom. It's been hard on her since my dad died."

"My mom, too, although she's had a long time to adjust to widowhood."

"Is your sister close?"

"A hundred miles away, but they get together often."

Ashley concentrated on her hands. "I didn't handle my dad's death well. Mom, either. I think if we'd had time to prepare, I mean, if he'd been sick for a long time, we might have been able to accept it." She paused and bit into her lower lip. "But one morning he kissed both mom and me goodbye, went to work, and by noon he was dead."

"Heart attack?"

She shook her head. "He worked on the docks. There was an accident and Dad was in the wrong place at the wrong time. It's been three years and it does get easier with time, but it's always there. It's worse for Mom than me. Dad was her soulmate. They were together constantly. Dad had such big plans for their retirement; he wanted to travel to every state in the union and had money set aside to buy a motor home. It was his dream."

"Life is like that, Ash," he said, his voice gentle, caring. "I saw more death than I ever cared to while in Afghanistan. I lost friends who had dreams of their own: wives, babies they had yet to hold."

"Is that why you left the military?"

"Part of the reason. When you ask if I have dreams, I can say that I do. I want to do my part to put an end to evil. I want to live the life my friends didn't get the chance to live and marry a woman I can love and trust, who will feel the same about me."

She knew he was thinking about the one who'd hurt him while he was away serving his country and the one who'd broken his heart that led to his enlistment. He'd never mentioned either name, and that was fine. She wanted Dash to concentrate on the future rather than on the past.

"And I want to go fly-fishing," Dash added.

"Fly-fishing?"

"Yeah, that was something my dad and I used to do. I haven't been able to in a long time . . . since shortly before Dad died when I was a teen. I've been feeling the urge to get out there and let go of my worries while I fished, just the way my dad did."

"There's great fly-fishing in the Pacific Northwest," she said, assuming he'd get the job. She wanted it for him and for herself, although there was no guarantee she'd find work close to Seattle.

"I'll keep that in mind," he said.

"My dad loved to fly-fish, too. There was nothing he enjoyed more than standing in the middle of some fast-moving stream in those ridiculous-looking rubber pants with suspenders and swinging his line. Watching him was amazing. I can still remember seeing that line swirl through the air with the same grace as a ballerina."

A slow smile crept over Dash's face. "That sounds pretty close to heaven to me."

Ashley's mind was filled with childhood memories of her father fishing and his love of the sport.

Dash frowned as he glanced in his rearview mirror. "I don't believe it," he said with a groan.

"Believe what?"

"I'm being pulled over again."

"The state patrol?" Ashley had a hard time believing it herself. Twice in one day had to be some kind of record.

"Not the state patrol. But it looks likes law enforcement to me."

Ashley glanced over her shoulder and caught sight of a large black Suburban tailing them, red lights flashing. A police car was behind him, and another car as well. It looked like an entire parade of law enforcement vehicles.

Dash slowed and then eased to a stop on the right-hand side of the freeway. The traffic on I-5 whizzed past as he reached over her for the paperwork for the rental car.

Ashley couldn't imagine what they could have possibly done to attract all this attention. Sure, someone had switched their license plates, but this had to be something else. Now what?

"What in the name of . . ." Dash's face hardened as he checked his rearview mirror. "Ashley, listen to me." His voice was low and hard. "Do whatever they say. Understand?"

"Yes, but . . ."

Before she could finish, the passenger door was jerked

open and a man stood on the other side with a gun pointed directly at her. She gasped and automatically raised her hands.

"Get out of the vehicle with your hands clasped behind your head." The man with the gun gestured for her to move.

She swallowed a sense of panic. "I . . . what about the dog?" Little Blade was asleep in her lap.

The plainclothes officer hesitated. "Keep your hands where I can see them."

Ashley did as instructed.

"Buckley, get the puppy."

Another man appeared and grabbed hold of Little Blade.

"There's a carrier in the backseat," Ashley told him. "It would be best if you'd put him in that for now."

Ashley could hear Dash arguing with another law enforcement official. He was already outside the vehicle and standing with his hands behind his head as he answered their questions. From his raised voice, it sounded as if he was about to lose his cool.

Once Ashley was free of the dog, she climbed out of the car with her hands tucked behind her head. "I can explain everything," she said, doing her best to remain calm despite the fact that her heart was pounding at an alarming rate. Glancing around, she was shocked to see about a dozen different men and women from a variety of official agencies, if their uniforms were anything to go by.

"Homeland Security?" she heard Dash shout. "You people must be crazy."

"On your knees," the man with the gun directed her.

Ashley looked down at the ground, which was soggy and slushy. "I'll get my jeans wet," she protested. "Couldn't you do whatever it is you have to do with me standing?"

"Handcuff her," the man with the gun ordered to the one he'd referred to as Buckley.

"Hey, that hurts! Wait a minute," she said, hardly able to believe what was happening. "You're going to handcuff me? Whatever for?" This was beyond the point of being ridiculous.

Buckley stepped forward and grabbed hold of her wrist and slapped on the handcuffs.

"I know my rights. I learned the Pledge of Allegiance," she said. "What about liberty and justice for all? What about my rights as an American?" The men weren't answering.

"Dash?" she cried out desperately, as they each held an arm and marched her toward the Suburban. "What's happening?"

"I don't know," he shouted back, and he seemed to be as bewildered as she was.

"Where are you taking me?" she demanded, struggling now. "I want an attorney. You're supposed to let me make a phone call."

She could hear Dash arguing with the police, and when she looked over her shoulder, she saw it took two men to restrain him.

"You're making a huge mistake," he insisted, but no one seemed to be listening.

"Bring him in, too," the man in charge shouted out.

"What about Little Blade?" she asked. They couldn't abandon the puppy. The poor dog would need counseling after being left behind once already. "Who's going to take care of the puppy?"

Buckley got her situated in the backseat of the Suburban, which wasn't an easy task with her hands locked behind her back. As soon as she was secured, he returned to the rental car.

The man who'd pointed the gun at her spoke: "I bet you thought you'd outsmarted us again."

Ashley had the feeling no amount of arguing was going to convince this hard-nosed enforcement officer that she was innocent of whatever he thought she had done. With that in mind, she kept her mouth shut. She wasn't stupid. She watched *NCIS* and a bunch of those cop shows. The more information she offered, the more she was likely to dig herself into a deep, dark hole.

"Not going to talk?"

She pinched her lips together just so he'd know she had no intention of explaining herself. "I want an attorney."

"You're under the jurisdiction of the FBI and Homeland Security, and you don't get to lawyer up until we say you do."

Ashley's mouth sagged open in shock. Her bottom lip started to tremble, but she wasn't about to give in to tears and emotion. This would all be straightened out soon enough. And when it was, she was determined to sue his sorry butt.

"What is your name?" she asked, ever so sweetly, because she intended to memorize it for when the time came to file a lawsuit against the federal government.

"Officer Jordan Wilkes at your service."

"You must be a direct descendant of John Wilkes Booth," she said without humor.

His smile was just short of maniacal. "As a matter of fact, there is a family link to the assassin who killed Abraham Lincoln."

"You say that with such pride, too," she scoffed, forgetting her earlier decision to remain silent.

Looking out the window, she noticed that Dash wasn't taking kindly to being restrained. He stepped back and shook his head, all the while arguing. Ashley could see he wasn't able to reason with them any better than she had. She didn't know what this was about, but she had a strong feeling she would soon find out.

When the man referred to as Buckley returned, he joined

Agent Wilkes in the front seat. With a motorcycle escort they eased back onto the freeway. As she passed Dash, he captured her gaze and offered her a small smile of reassurance. In those brief seconds he seemed to be telling her that no matter what happened, he'd get this resolved.

Once back on the freeway, an escort led the way to Eugene, Oregon. They traveled with lights flashing, as if this was a motorcade with some high-ranking dignitary. Ashley wasn't fooled—she could tell she wasn't going to be treated like royalty. Still, she remained completely oblivious as to what she'd done or was suspected of having done to warrant all this attention.

They arrived at what she could only assume was a police station. Ashley was helped out of the car and led down a long, narrow hallway to an interrogation room. Once inside, her hands were freed and she was left alone.

Left alone for hours . . . or what seemed like hours.

This happened in the procedural shows she routinely watched, so it wasn't completely unexpected. Still, it played with her mind, which she supposed was the purpose. She sat tense and apprehensive, wondering about Dash and Little Blade. In an effort to calm her nerves, she closed her eyes and remembered the look that had come over Dash's face just before he leaned in and kissed her the last time. The memory produced a lazy, happy smile.

As time progressed, Ashley grew worried. If the authorities detained him, he might miss his interview. She couldn't think about that. She could only hope that he'd be released soon so he could get to Seattle on time.

After what seemed like endless hours, Ashley lost track of how long she'd been left alone in the room. She suspected it was late into the afternoon when Agent Wilkes stepped in, holding a pad and pen just the way Gibbs did in *NCIS*.

He pulled out the chair, causing the legs to make a scraping sound against the concrete floor. This was probably an intimidation tactic.

Ashley resisted telling him she was onto his game. Instead, she smiled calmly, letting him know she wasn't the least bit nervous. Eventually, Agent Wilkes would be forced to admit he was in the wrong. Leaning back in her chair, she stretched out her arms and clasped her hands together on top of the table.

She waited for him to speak first. He didn't. Instead, he made an elaborate show of taking off his watch and setting it on the table. Apparently, he was timing her answers.

When he spoke his voice was curt. "Name."

"That which is usually given to a child at birth," she replied, saying the first thing that came to mind.

He was not amused. "What is your name?"

"It's on my driver's license in my purse, which you have confiscated."

"Humor me. What is your name?"

"Ashley Gene Davison."

He cracked a smile as if he'd caught her in a lie.

"And that's Gene with a *G* rather than a *J*." This small detail had caused her untold troubles since the time she started school.

"Isn't that rather unusual?"

She was convinced that the more the agent got her to talk, the more likely she was to make a mistake.

Ashley hesitated, unsure it was wise to explain herself. "My middle name is spelled *G-E-N-E*. I was supposed to be a boy and my dad promised my uncle he would name his baby after him, so it's spelled in the masculine form."

Wilkes made a notation on the tablet, but it was clear he didn't believe her.

"Your home address."

"Seattle or California?"

"Either."

She complied with both. "Can I ask you a question?"

He glanced up from the tablet but didn't answer.

"Where are Dash and Little Blade? Dash has an important interview this afternoon. He needs to be in Seattle. Can you make that happen?"

"Your hostage is being debriefed."

"Debriefed?" she repeated, and then half rose from the table as his words connected with her brain. "My hostage?"

Chapter Seventeen

"Are you people out of your minds?" Dash demanded, glaring across the table at Wilkes. "How many times do I have to tell you I am not a hostage."

Wilkes didn't respond. Agent Buckley was on the other side of the two-way mirror, taking in Wilkes's interviewing techniques. The young agent had a lot to learn, but he was coming along nicely.

Wilkes didn't feel the need to respond to Sutherland's question. He actually felt sorry for Dashiell Sutherland. The man didn't have a clue of the danger he'd been in, nor did he realize he'd been a pawn for one of the deadliest criminals on the FBI Most Wanted list.

After interviewing Ashley Davison for nearly two frustrating hours, he'd set about getting the information he needed from Sutherland.

Wilkes remained undaunted. Davison had adamantly insisted she wasn't the woman he sought. He had to admit she sounded believable, which only went to prove how good she was. She came off as sincere and honest. A less-experienced agent might be tempted to believe her.

It was only a matter of time before she cracked, and crack she would, but it would take diligence and expertise for that. Wilkes felt equal to the challenge.

"Can you explain again about the loss of your phone?" Wilkes asked, ever patient and in control.

"Losing my phone was an accident," Sutherland insisted. "I put it inside my coat pocket and then tossed it into the backseat. As best I can figure, that's when it fell out of the car."

"Were you distracted?"

"What do you mean by *distracted*?" The other man's eyes narrowed with the question.

Wilkes explained, "Did Ms. Davison do anything to avert your attention?"

"No," he returned, with more than a hint of defiance. "Would you listen to me? Losing the phone was an accident."

"Did she flirt with you?"

"When?"

"When you put your coat in the car," Wilkes asked.

"Hardly," Sutherland said, and then smiled. His look had been angry and defensive just seconds earlier, and the sudden transformation came as a shock.

"You find that humorous?"

"Actually, I do. Ashley was convinced she couldn't trust me. It was only after she spoke with my mother and got reassurances that I wasn't a serial killer that she even agreed to share the car with me. Trust me, there was no flirting from either one of us. I was annoyed by her—she was annoyed by me."

Again, Wilkes had to admit that the woman was brilliant. She'd managed to kidnap this man—a former army intelligence officer, no less—and convinced him that she was nothing more than a starving grad student. She even had him believing she was headed to Seattle for Christmas with her widowed mother. He grudgingly had to admire such talent.

"What can you tell me about the dog?"

"What's there to tell that I haven't already explained to the other officer? The puppies were abandoned at the rest stop. Ashley decided to rescue one and give it to her mother as a Christmas gift."

"And you believed her?"

"Is there a reason I shouldn't?"

Wilkes saw no need to answer. The poor guy was delusional. Wilkes actually felt sorry for him. He'd been duped by a master.

"Okay," Sutherland said with exaggerated patience. "I left Ashley in the rest stop parking lot. If she was a criminal mastermind, the way you claim, do you seriously think she would have let me drive off?" He held his hands palms up, as if to say what Wilkes had suggested was utter nonsense.

And it was true, Ashley Davison had taken a gamble, letting Sutherland voluntarily leave. But by that time she'd managed to play on Dash Sutherland's generous nature. She'd been able to convince him that returning to the rest stop for her and the dog was all his idea. Wilkes still didn't know how the puppy played into this scenario, but he'd find out eventually. The dog was a sweet one, and it curdled his stomach to imagine what twisted plan this evil woman had set in motion.

Wilkes studied Sutherland sitting across from him and asked what should have been obvious: "Did you ever consider the fact that she knew you'd eventually return for her and the puppy?"

"How could she?" Dash asked defiantly. "I didn't know it. I had no intention of turning around until my conscience demanded that I not leave her. She would have been stuck there. Listen," he continued, forcefully expelling his breath in an apparent effort to control his temper. "I spent the last four years in army intelligence. I'm a good judge of character, and I'm telling you this woman is no criminal mastermind."

Wilkes appreciated the other man's sincerity, but clearly Sutherland didn't have a clue.

"What about the license plates—"

"Some kids were responsible for that," the other man broke in. "We actually spoke to them, although we didn't realize what they'd done at the time."

"You say she couldn't have arranged switching license plates in advance?"

"How could she?" He tossed his hands up in what looked like abject frustration.

"You were together every minute?" Wilkes didn't know how she'd done it, but she had arranged the switch. There could be no question that she'd somehow set it up in advance.

"Ash and I were together almost every minute."

That was all Wilkes needed to know. "Are you saying that it's out of the realm of possibility that she orchestrated it beforehand?"

"Yes. For you to even suggest it tells me you don't know what you're talking about. Ashley had no idea where we were going to stop or how long we'd be inside the building."

"She could have had you followed."

"That's a possibility," he conceded, sitting back and crossing his arms over his chest. At last Wilkes was getting somewhere. As with most interrogations, the suspect had started to crack. Wilkes had actually thought it would take longer, seeing that Sutherland had been in the military.

"You're right," Sutherland said. "It is possible, but it didn't happen. You have the wrong woman."

So breaking Dash Sutherland wasn't going to be nearly as easy as Wilkes had hoped. With a flash of insight, he understood why.

"You're falling in love with her, aren't you?"

Sutherland jerked his head up and pinched his lips together.

Wilkes thought so.

"She's got you wrapped around her little finger. That didn't take long, did it? She batted her eyelashes at you and within a matter of hours you were under her control."

Sutherland's eyes held fire as he glared back at him.

"You were her pawn and you fell neatly into that role."

Dash jumped to his feet. "You're full of it, Agent Wilkes. Ashley is no more a criminal mastermind than I am. She's a graduate student and a wonderful, caring woman who loves her family. You are so off base it sickens me."

Wilkes had thought to anger the other man and Sutherland had taken the bait. Wilkes had gotten the reaction he'd hoped to achieve.

"So you are in love with her."

"My feelings for Ashley don't come into play here."

"You're wrong," Wilkes said, coming to his feet as well. "Sit down, Sutherland." He waited until the other man reclaimed his seat, and then Wilkes left the room.

Agent Buckley met him on the other side of the door. "Sutherland is clearly convinced we have the wrong woman," he said, and from the way he said it, Wilkes thought the junior agent agreed.

"I have two words for you," Wilkes said: "Stockholm syndrome."

"What?"

"The term comes from an incident that happened back in the seventies, when bank robbers held hostages for several days. By the time they were rescued, the hostages were fighting the police in order to protect the robbers. In the end, one of the women actually became engaged to one of the men. And don't forget Patty Hearst."

"I know what Stockholm syndrome is. Do you really think Dashiell Sutherland is suffering from it?"

"He clearly has deep feelings for her." Wilkes decided to test his theory. "Let me try something."

"Okay."

Wilkes returned to the other room. Sutherland regarded him with brooding eyes.

"I believe you've answered all our questions, Mr. Sutherland. You're free to go."

Sutherland shook his head. "I'm not leaving here without Ashley and the puppy. Then and only then will I leave this building."

Wilkes smiled. The other man's response told him everything he needed to know.

Chapter Eighteen

Ashley had been awake all night and was at the point of mental and physical exhaustion. Even now, she couldn't understand how she'd managed to walk into this nightmare. Nothing made sense. And worse, no matter how adamantly she'd declared her innocence, she hadn't been able to convince Agent Wilkes that she wasn't the dangerous felon on the FBI's Most Wanted list. By the time morning, or what she assumed was morning, had rolled around, she was dopey and distraught.

She was alone now. She'd asked about Dash and Little Blade several times, but no one would volunteer any information. She had to assume the puppy was also in a holding cell. She prayed that Dash had been released and had left for Seattle in enough time to make his interview. It was difficult to keep her spirits up and not dissolve into tears. This had to be the worst Christmas of her life. And now—and this was even worse—no one was talking to her. Alone in a cell, she had nothing to do but dwell on the injustice of it all.

Ashley laid her head down on the bed and closed her eyes, only to hear the outer door open. When she looked up she saw Agent Buckley. She liked him better than the older agent, who kept insisting she wasn't a grad student but a despicable felon intent on terrorist activity.

"How are you holding up?" Buckley asked.

Her eyes had blurred from lack of sleep. "Okay, I guess." But she wasn't okay. She was sad and miserable, and she wanted her mother.

"Well, I have news that should cheer you up," Agent Buckley said, offering her a smile. "You're free to go."

Ashley leaped off the bed as if someone had lit it on fire. She rushed to the door. "You believe me? You know who I really am? What happened to change your mind?"

"It only took a few minutes to verify your story. Unfortunately, Agent Wilkes refused to believe it."

"Is that the commotion I heard?" At one point, Ashley had heard arguing, lots of arguing. The loudest voice seemed to be Agent Wilkes's. He'd kept insisting he knew what he was doing and warning the others not to be fooled. Ashley had been afraid to hope that his colleagues were unconvinced.

"I'm afraid Agent Wilkes had something of a mental collapse. He'll be taking a leave of absence from the bureau."

Ashley supposed if she were a better person she'd feel sorry about that. But after this ordeal that might have even cost Dash a possible job, she couldn't pretend she did.

"We have confirmation that the Ashley Davison we want is in Mexico."

"That's good to know."

"All your personal items will be returned to you in short order."

"Thank you," Ashley said, doing her best to smile. Her biggest concerns—well, other than Dash and the puppy— were her purse and coat. "What about Little Blade?"

The agent escorted her past a long line of locked cell doors. "I believe the puppy is currently with Mr. Sutherland."

"Oh." She did her best to hold back the urge to weep. That meant she was truly alone now. Dash had Little Blade with him, and the two were on their way to Seattle. Worrying about the puppy was only a small part of her problem, however. Ashley was stuck in Eugene, Oregon, with no way of getting to Seattle.

Being led to the front of the building, it didn't take long for her to sign off on her personal items. Once she had her coat and purse, she was released into a foyer. With her head hanging low, and holding back tears, she stepped into the room. The first thing she noticed was that it was snowing again, giant flakes coming down outside the lobby windows. She turned back to ask about where she might catch a bus to Seattle, when she heard her name.

"Ashley."

On the far side of the room sat Dash. He had Little Blade with him, and the puppy was on a leash. For one wild moment all she could do was stare in disbelief. Without thought, Ashley raced across the room and threw herself into Dash's arms. Never in all her life had she been happier to see anyone.

"What are you doing here?" she asked, hugging him so close it was a wonder Dash could breathe. "What about your interview? You should be in Seattle. Did you come back for me?" She didn't give him time to answer. Instead, she was kissing his beautiful face, so happy to see him that she was beyond self-restraint.

It didn't take Dash long to take hold of her head and to kiss her back, hugging her with the same intensity with which she held on to him.

Agent Buckley stood in the background, and after several minutes cleared his throat.

Ashley reluctantly broke off the kiss and looked over her shoulder to the FBI agent.

"You wanted something?" Dash asked, tightening his hold on Ashley, as if to protect her. His grip told her he wasn't going to let anyone take her out of his arms.

"I just wanted to wish you both a merry Christmas."

"Thank you," Ashley said, feeling a hundred times better already. Picking up Little Blade, she lavished attention on the puppy and hugged him close to her face, grateful that he was safe and well. She'd missed him and Dash like crazy.

It was hard to believe she'd been in custody twenty-four hours when it'd felt like a lifetime. Even now, she wasn't sure how her identity had been verified, only that it had. It'd all been a terrible misunderstanding.

The agent left and Dash led Ashley outside and into the falling snow. Tilting her head back, she looked up at the sky and smiled until she remembered Dash hadn't answered her questions about the interview. Tucking her hands on each side of his face, she held his eyes with her own.

"What about the job interview?"

"I didn't make it."

She dropped her gaze, feeling dreadful. Dash kissed her nose. "No worries, Ash. There will be others."

"But this job was perfect."

He didn't argue with her. "It is what it is. Even if they

had released me in time, there was no way was I going to abandon you until this mess was straightened out."

"I would have found a way to get to Seattle."

"I didn't care how long the FBI held you," Dash insisted. "I wasn't leaving without you."

"But . . ."

"I agreed to share the car with you all the way to Seattle. I wasn't going back on my word."

"But . . ."

"Are you disappointed I'm here?" he asked, arching his thick brows with the question.

In response, she buried her face in his coat and hugged him again. "No, oh Dash, never. I just hate the thought of you missing out on this job because of me."

"I called the company and offered my apologies."

"And?" she asked, looking up at him, certain her eyes must be full of hope.

"And they thanked me for letting them know."

"That was it?" She could hear the disappointment in his voice.

He nodded. "Like I said, there will be other job interviews. It wasn't meant to be. Please don't think twice about it. I've put it out of my mind and so should you."

"I'll try, but I don't know that I'll be able to." Her heart was heavy, knowing that he'd given up this opportunity in order to help her.

"Come on," he said, slipping his arm around her waist and leading her toward the parking lot.

The falling snow was so beautiful it took her breath away. Her father used to say that snow came from angels scattering dust from the sky. That's exactly how this felt. She inhaled, taking in how wonderful it felt to be in the open air with this man at her side.

"Let's get to Seattle before something else delays us."

"Who would have ever thought it would be this complicated to drive from San Francisco to Seattle?" she whispered, on the tail end of a yawn. "Did you get any sleep last night?" she asked, covering her mouth and yawning a second time.

"Some. Did you?"

"None. I've never been in jail before. I don't recommend the accommodations."

Dash grinned and kissed her before opening the passenger door. He paused, his hand on the car door. "Agent Wilkes claimed I'd fallen in love with you and that you'd twisted my thinking."

"He didn't!" Ashley was outraged on Dash's behalf. This was too much, but then she wondered how he'd answered. Biting down on her lower lip, she toyed with asking him.

"Wilkes was quite insistent that I'd been taken in by your good-girl act and lost perspective."

"Were you?" she asked in a small voice, curious about how he'd responded.

"I'm afraid so. Ashley, I'm crazy about you."

Now she knew she was going to cry.

"I'd have to be, to put up with everything that's taken place in the last forty-eight hours. There was no way I was leaving Eugene without you. I called every attorney in the phone book, I contacted Amnesty International and every other agency I could think of that might help. I became a blathering idiot over you and I'd do it again, if I thought it would help."

"Oh Dash, I'm nuts about you, too. Are we crazy?" She wondered if either one of them was thinking straight, considering they were both sleep-deprived.

"I think we must be," he agreed. That said, he looked down on her with a big smile on his face. "Still, I wouldn't change a thing—about you, about this crazy drive, about Little Blade, or a single other thing that's happened. Well, maybe other than you spending time in the slammer."

After closing her door, Dash walked around the car, climbed in the driver's seat, and started the engine.

"No wonder I'm so attracted to you." Ashley smiled over at him and then leaned her head against the back of the seat. Little Blade was in her lap, his chin on her knee.

Dash reached for her hand and gave it a gentle squeeze.

They talked, keeping each other awake for the remainder of the drive into Seattle. They hit heavy traffic outside of Tacoma, but it didn't bother them. They were high on simply being together.

When Dash parked in front of Ashley's family home, he grew quiet.

"You go inside and greet your mother."

"You're coming, too, aren't you?" she questioned.

"Not now."

"Dash, we have plenty of room and you're welcome to spend the night."

"I want you to take this time with your mother, okay? I'll be by later."

"Promise?"

He leaned over and kissed her. "Promise," he said.

If Ashley knew anything about Dash Sutherland, it was the fact that he was a man of his word. If he made a promise, he kept it.

Chapter Nineteen

Ashley rang the doorbell and waited. This was the moment she'd held in her mind since she'd gotten word that she had the time off.

She heard her mother walking toward the door, muttering something like "Hold your horses, I'm coming."

Sallie Davison opened the front door and blinked twice before she shouted, "Ashley Gene." She threw open her arms and grabbed hold of her in a hug that was strong enough to crack her ribs.

"Merry Christmas, Mom."

"How . . . when?" Her mother brought her into the house, but continued to stare at her as if she feared Ashley was a vision and would disappear as unexpectedly as she'd appeared.

"The diner closed for repairs," Ashley explained, "and I decided to head home and surprise you."

"And who is this?" she asked, leaning down to pet Little Blade.

"He's one of your Christmas gifts."

"Ashley Gene," her mother whispered, and covered her mouth as tears blurred her eyes.

"Mom, I've got so much to tell you, but I'm dead on my feet. I need a shower and a nap before I feel human again. Oh, and Mom, I met the most wonderful man. We rode up from San Francisco together and I'm crazy about him." She paused and studied her mother. "Is it possible to fall in love with someone after only two days?"

Her mother cupped Ashley's face and smiled. "It happened to your father and me. We met just as he was about to ship out with the navy and were together only two days."

"Oh Mom, I have so much to tell you . . ." The last part escaped on a loud yawn.

"Where is this young man of yours?"

"He'll be back, but for right now I think he went to buy a phone. You see, he lost his . . . I'll explain later, okay?"

Her mother followed her up the stairs and Ashley talked nonstop about Dash and their wild adventures on the drive from San Francisco, until it felt as if she was about to collapse from lack of sleep.

As it happened, Ashley slept through the afternoon and the night, and didn't wake until seven in the morning on Christmas Eve.

Ashley came down the stairs still groggy but well rested. She kept her phone close at hand, expecting to hear from Dash at any moment—well, maybe not quite this early, but soon. She found her mother busy in the kitchen, getting everything ready for their dinner that evening.

"I still can't believe you're here," Sallie Davison said as she poured a cup of coffee for Ashley and delivered it to the table.

Ashley was scrunched up on the chair, her knees tucked up under her chin, as she cradled the mug in her hands. "I can't believe it, either," she murmured, reveling in her first cup of the day. "Oh Mom, it was a crazy, unbelievable drive. I can't wait for you to meet Dash."

"I can't wait to meet him, either. From the minute you walked in the door, he was all you could talk about, and frankly, Ashley, you weren't making a lot of sense."

That didn't surprise her. Not more than an hour after she'd arrived, Ashley had completely zonked out.

Her mother placed an English muffin in front of Ashley, then sat down at the table across from her.

Ashley finished off the English muffin, wiping a smear of peanut butter off the corner of her mouth. "I'm going to go upstairs and get dressed." She hoped that by the time she finished, Dash would be stopping by.

"I'm running to the grocery store," her mother shouted up the stairs after her.

"Mom, you don't need to fix a fancy dinner, you know."

"It's Christmas Eve, and . . ." She hesitated. "Actually, I should probably tell you now."

"Tell me what?" Ashley asked, standing at the top of the stairs and looking down on her mother.

"I invited a man to dinner."

"Oh? Who?"

"You've never met him."

This was an interesting development and a surprise. "Who is he, Mom?"

Making a dismissive gesture, her mother said, "Now, I don't want you making more of this than warranted. His name is Cole and he's a widower. I met him while volunteering at the library. He volunteers, too. His children live in other states, and since I was going to be alone for Christmas and he was, too, we decided to celebrate the holidays together."

Ashley was pleased for her mother. "That's wonderful, Mom."

Her mother refused to make eye contact. "You don't mind?"

"Of course not. Why would I mind? How long have the two of you been . . . dating?"

"Not long. About two months now. We aren't sleeping together, if that concerns you."

"Mom. TMI. This is your life. What you and Cole do is your own business."

Her mother's smile was shy and sweet, as if she was deeply relieved to have told Ashley about her man friend.

Her mother left, and in an effort to kill time before Dash arrived, she decided to bake cookies. She chose Mexican wedding cakes, the very ones he'd mentioned that he enjoyed. The cookies were baked and set aside when the doorbell chimed.

With her heart in her throat, Ashley hurried to the living room and threw open the door without looking to see who it might be. Dash stood on the other side, holding a poinsettia plant in one hand.

Ashley took it out of his hands and then leaped into his arms. "Merry Christmas, Dash."

Hugging her with his arms around her waist, Dash whirled her around. Laughing, Ashley wrapped her legs around his waist and captured his mouth with her own. The twirling stopped as they both became deeply involved in the kiss. They'd been apart only a handful of hours, but Ashley had missed him dreadfully. She told him so with her lips and he responded with equal fervor.

Little Blade bounded into the living room and barked excitedly.

Breaking off the kiss, Dash looked down at the puppy. "Looks like Little Blade missed me, too."

"We both did," Ashley assured him, twining her arms around his neck. "But I missed you more." She pressed the side of her head against his shoulder.

Reluctantly, Dash released her. "As soon as I left you yesterday afternoon, I picked up a new phone. It drove me crazy not to have my cell."

"You didn't call me?"

He traced his finger down the side of her face. "I didn't know your number, which I found frustrating as hell. If I'd been thinking, I would have gotten it earlier."

With their arms around each other, Ashley led him into the kitchen.

"Where's your mother?" he asked.

"The store, and guess what? My mother has a man friend. He's joining us for dinner, and . . . would you mind very much if I called and talked to your mother again?"

Dash's head came back. "You want to talk to my mother? Is there any particular reason?"

"I want to let her know she raised an honorable man and

that I'm seriously taking into consideration what she told me."

"Which is?" he asked with arched brows.

"Between your mother and me."

"Okay, but I think you should know I made a decision last night."

He sounded serious. "Which is?"

"I'm going to look for a job in the San Francisco area. We've just gotten to know each other and I want to give us a chance."

"I want to give us a chance, too."

"I'm looking for a position as a consultant. I should be able to find enough work to keep me afloat until you graduate. If this thing between us works out the way I hope it does, then we can both move to Seattle."

Ashley stared back at him, hardly able to believe Dash was willing to change his plans for her.

Who would have believed that only three days ago she'd been frustrated because she'd been unable to fly home? Her plans had been thwarted in the most surprising of ways. Instead, she'd found herself dashing through the snow in a twist of fate that led her to Dash.

Her arms were securely wrapped around him and they continued kissing until Dash reluctantly broke off the heady exchange.

Ashley followed his gaze and looked over her shoulder

to discover her mother standing in the doorway, her arms loaded down with groceries. Right away, Dash went to help.

"You must be Dash," her mother said, coming into the house.

"I am, and in case you didn't know, I'm pretty much crazy about your daughter."

"So she says," Sallie Davison said, smiling. "And she also tells me she feels the same about you."

Dash brushed the hair from Ashley's brow. "Good thing," he whispered, his eyes boring into her.

"It is a very good thing," Ashley agreed, and not caring that her mother was watching, she leaned forward and kissed Dash again. Ah yes, this was going to be a great Christmas after all.

Beloved author Debbie Macomber celebrates the most
wonderful time of the year in her heartwarming
Christmas novel of romance, hope,
and the comforts of home.

Mr. Miracle

Available from Ballantine Books
Continue reading for a sneak peek.

Chapter One

This wasn't the way it was supposed to happen. Six years out of high school, Addie Folsom had envisioned returning home loaded and driving a fancy car. Instead, she was limping back in a twenty-year-old Honda with close to three hundred thousand miles and her tail between her legs.

So much for the great promise of moving to Montana and walking into a get-rich-quick opportunity. She'd left Washington State with such high hopes . . . and ended up living in a leaky trailer and waiting tables in a run-down diner. It took all six of those years for Addie to admit she'd made a very big mistake. Pride, she'd learned, offered little comfort.

Oh, she'd returned home for visits at least a couple of times a year. When asked pointed questions about her work in the silver mine, she'd made sure her answers were vague.

Then, last summer, her chiropractor father had died unexpectedly of a heart attack.

Addie had adored her dad as a child, but the moment she'd hit her teen years, their relationship had deteriorated. She hadn't repaired things before he'd passed away so suddenly. In retrospect, she suspected she and her father were too much alike. Both were stubborn and headstrong, unwilling to admit when they were wrong or make the effort to build bridges.

They'd argued far too often, her mother stepping in, seeking to make peace between her husband and her daughter. How sorry Addie was for the strife between them, now that her father was gone.

For now, she was home for good. Addie parked in front of the single-story house where she'd spent the first eighteen years of her life. She loved that it had a front porch, which so many of the more modern homes didn't. Normally, the Christmas lights would already be up. Her father had always seen to that the Friday after Thanksgiving. This year, however, the two arborvitae that bordered each side of the porch seemed stark and bare without the decorative lights.

Her mother must have been watching from the living-room window, because the minute Addie climbed out of the car, the front door flew open and Sharon Folsom rushed out with her arms open wide. "Addie, Addie, you're home."

Addie paused halfway up the walkway and hugged her mother close.

Sharon Folsom brought her hands up to Addie's face and smoothed back her dark brown hair. Her mother's chocolate-brown eyes, a reflection of her own, held her gaze with an intensity of longing.

Addie found she couldn't speak. It felt so good to be home, to really be home.

Her mother hugged her even tighter this time. "You said you were coming back, and I'd hoped . . ." She left the rest unsaid.

"I'm not returning to Montana this time, Mom."

"Oh Addie, really? I couldn't be happier. So you decided you are definitely back to stay?" She wrapped her arm around Addie's waist and led her up the porch steps. "It's so wonderful to have you home, especially at this time of year . . . it's the first one that's so difficult, you know."

The first Christmas without Dad.

"I talked to your uncle Roy," her mother said.

"Yes?" Addie tried hard not to show how anxious she was to hear what her mother had found out.

"He's pleased to know you're interested in health care. Your dad would have been so happy; that was what he always wanted for you. Roy said once you get your high school diploma, he'll do everything within his power to get you the schooling you need. He's even willing to hire you part-time while you're in school and to work around your class schedule."

Addie hardly knew what to say. This was an opportunity she had never expected. More than she could ever hope would happen. Now it was up to her not to blow it.

"Aren't you excited?"

Again, her throat tightened and she answered with a sharp nod. She knew that no matter what she hoped to accomplish, she'd need her high school diploma. One class credit was all she needed. Why she'd dropped out when she was so close to graduation was beyond her. How stupid and shortsighted she'd been. Her one missing credit was in literature, so she'd found a class she could take at the local community college.

B-o-r-i-n-g!

As a high school sophomore, Addie had been assigned *Moby-Dick* to read. Because of her dyslexia, she was a slow, thoughtful reader, often using her finger on the page to help her keep track of the words. Then to be handed that doorstop and work her way through it page by excruciating page had been pure torture. Following *Moby-Dick,* she'd been completely turned off to reading in general . . . although lately, after her television had stopped working, she'd gotten a couple of books at the library and enjoyed them immensely. Finding pleasure in reading had given her hope that maybe . . . just maybe she could return to school.

"I already signed up for a literature class. It starts this week, which I understand is a bit unusual; apparently, it was delayed until a teacher could be replaced." Addie had thought she'd need to wait until mid-February, when the second semester began. This class was perfectly timed for her.

"You enrolled already?" How pleased her mother sounded, and her face brightened with the news.

They were inside the house now, and after removing her coat, Addie tucked her fingertips in the back pockets of her jeans. Standing in the middle of the kitchen, she looked around and breathed in the welcome she found in the familiar setting. Her mother had placed a few festive things around the house to help celebrate the season. The Advent wreath rested in the center of the kitchen table. The first purple candle had been lit.

When she was growing up, it'd been a big deal to see who got to light the candle every night at dinner, Addie or her brother. Generally, Jerry was given the honor. Oh, how her brother had loved lording it over her. He lived in Oklahoma now, was married, and worked as a physical therapist for a center that trained Olympic athletes. He'd always been athletic himself, just like his best friend, Erich Simmons, who lived next door. The two had been inseparable;

any mental image of her brother also conjured up his constant sidekick and the way she'd humiliated herself over Erich.

At one time Addie had thought Erich Simmons was the cutest boy in the universe. He was a star athlete, class valedictorian, and the homecoming king. Addie hadn't thought of him in a long time and didn't know why he'd popped into her head now. As a teen, she'd idolized Erich and hadn't bothered to hide the way she felt. He, unfortunately, found her hero worship highly amusing. Oh, there'd been the usual antics when they were kids. Her brother and Erich had wanted nothing to do with her, despite all her efforts to follow them around. It wasn't until she was fourteen and fifteen that she'd viewed Erich in a different light and sent him valentines and baked him cookies. It embarrassed her no end to remember what a fool she'd made of herself over him, especially since he treated her like a jerk.

"Addie?" Her mother broke into her thoughts. "You look a million miles away."

"Sorry, Mom."

"Bring in your suitcases. I've got your old room all ready for you."

It felt wonderful to be home.

Addie unloaded her car, which, sadly, took only a few minutes. Everything she'd managed to accumulate in six years was contained in two suitcases and a couple of boxes.

When she finished unpacking, she headed directly for the garage.

Her mother found her there ten minutes later. "Addie, my goodness, what are you doing here?" she asked. "I've been looking all over the house for you. Are you hungry? Would you like me to fix you something to eat?"

"In a little while."

"What are you doing?"

Addie stood in the middle of the garage, surrounded by several clear plastic boxes she'd brought down from the shelves. Her father had been a whiz at organization, a trait she'd inherited. "I'm looking for the outdoor Christmas lights."

"But, Addie—"

"It won't feel like Christmas without the trees by the porch lit up."

"But Addie—"

"Mom, please, let me put up the lights." Her dad would have wanted her to do this for her mother, Addie was sure. She owed him this, even if things hadn't been so good between them when he died, or maybe because of that.

"Erich offered to put them up for me, but I said no."

"Good." Perfect Erich. She bristled at the mere mention of his name. He'd always been so thoughtful and kind . . . to others. But he'd tortured her at every opportunity. For one thing, from the time they were in first grade together, he'd insisted on calling her Adeline. Addie had always hated the name. She'd never even known the great-grandmother she'd been named after. Saddling her with that name had been her father's doing, no surprise.

Her mother moved a couple of steps into the garage. "Um . . . there's a reason I didn't want Erich to put up the lights."

Addie straightened. Her mother's voice revealed hesitation and a bit of apprehension. "What is it, Mom?"

"I mentioned all those firsts without your father, remember . . . ?"

"Yes." It was one of the reasons Addie had returned home when she did. She didn't want her mother spending this first Christmas without Dad by herself. Jerry couldn't get away, but Addie could. Actually, she'd been more than ready to leave Montana. Although she'd come to love the state, everything else there had proved to be less perfect than she'd hoped. Her job at the mine had fizzled out after a few months, but pride hadn't allowed her to return home so soon after her grand departure. For a while she drifted from job to job, until finally settling in at the diner. She'd made friends and the tips were good. It was easy enough to coast through the next few years.

"I didn't say anything earlier when you called to say you were coming . . ." her mother said, interrupting her thoughts. Her mother wrung her hands.

"Mom, what is it?" Clearly there was something her mother didn't want to tell her.

"Please don't be upset with me."

This was all very strange. "Mom, please, don't worry. You're not going to upset me."

"You're sure?"

"Positive. Just tell me."

Her mother squeezed her eyes tightly shut. "I'm going on a two-week Christmas cruise with Julie Simmons."

It took a second for the information to sink in. "A cruise?"

Her mother still hadn't opened her eyes. "Julie's a widow. I'm a widow. We figured that we'd both get away this Christmas with a trip to the Caribbean. We booked a few days in Florida before the cruise as well. The sunshine and all . . . please tell me you're not upset with me."

"Of course not," Addie assured her, although her heart sank. This meant she'd be spending Christmas alone.

"Julie and I talked about it for months, and then right before Halloween we found this great deal from the cruise line and Julie said we should do it. If not now, when? I had no idea you'd be coming home, let alone for good, and . . . and, oh Addie, if you want I'll cancel the trip." Her voice became half plea and half regret.

"No way," Addie insisted, strengthening her resolve. "You're going on that cruise and you're going to enjoy every minute of it while I hold down the fort here."

"Erich offered to look after the house."

Of course he would.

"He's not married, you know, and neither is Karl."

Erich's younger brother.

As if she felt the need to keep talking, her mother continued. "Karl is dating a wonderful young woman and is spending Christmas with her family someplace back east. Neither Julie nor I have grandchildren yet, and being this has been such a difficult year . . ."

"Mom, please, you don't need to make excuses. I want you to do this. Please go."

"But you'll be alone."

"It's fine. I'll connect with a few friends and it won't be a problem. Don't worry about me."

"You're sure . . . ?"

"Absolutely positive."

"It's just that Julie and I have been so looking forward to this, and . . ."

Addie walked over and hugged her mother. "Stop. I wouldn't dream of letting you cancel this trip. It's perfect. You and Julie together on those warm sandy beaches. I'll be fine, I promise."

The relief in her mother's face was nearly palpable. Addie was sincere. She wanted her mother to get away for Christmas. "I still want to put up the outdoor lights," she said, returning to the plastic boxes her father had packed up the Christmas before and stored away.

"Oh sure, sweetheart, if that's what you want. Do you need me to help you?"

"I can do it." Among all the other valuable life lessons Montana had taught Addie, she'd learned resourcefulness. Though she'd never done it before, she'd figure out a way to string the lights on those two trees. It wouldn't feel like Christmas without them.

"I'll start dinner, then."

"Great. I'm starving."

After her mother left, Addie found the strands of outdoor lights and carted them to the front of the house. She needed a ladder, too. At five-foot-three, she wasn't nearly tall enough to reach the top.

She'd gotten everything set up when she heard the sound of a car door behind her. Standing halfway up the ladder, she glanced over her shoulder to see a bright, shiny, silver BMW parked at the curb behind her dilapidated, fender-rusting, once-blue Honda.

Erich.

Her heart sank. He was sure to make some derogatory comment about her car, right after he called her Adeline. He might even be so obnoxious as to mention her girlhood crush on him. Even before he spoke, her teeth were clenched.

"Adeline, is that you?"

Unbelievable! "It's Addie," she said coolly.

"Oops, sorry, I forgot," he teased, when clearly he hadn't. Then he had the audacity to laugh.

She brushed a long strand of dark hair away from her face.

"Need any help with that?"

"No, thanks," she said, as she continued to wind the strand around the bushy tree. She needed no help, least of all from him. It wasn't only the teasing she'd taken as a kid that contributed to her dislike of him—that was only a small part. Erich, Karl, and her brother had often ganged up on her. Being something of a tomboy, she'd followed them, hungering to join in their fun. Instead, Erich had teased her mercilessly. It'd gotten worse as she grew older and got braces. He'd called her "live wire" and poked fun at her until she'd run and hide in her bedroom. But that was nothing compared to the way he'd stepped all over her tender, young heart.

"You home for Christmas?" he asked.

"Something like that," she answered, without looking at him.

He hesitated, and when he spoke he sounded genuine and sincere. "Like I said when we spoke at the funeral, I'm sorry for your loss. I loved your dad."

"Yeah, me, too." The lump was back and she swallowed

hard, determined not to let him see how his words had affected her. Funny thing was, she didn't remember speaking to him at the funeral. She'd been in a fog then, confused and grieving.

"Maybe I'll see you around."

"Maybe," she returned dismissively. At the moment, all she wanted was for him to leave her alone.

By the time she had the lights wound around the first tree it was pitch-dark. The only illumination came from the porch light.

A little while later, when Addie was half finished with the twin tree on the other side of the porch, her mother opened the door and called out, "Dinner's ready."

"I'm almost done," Addie promised, unwilling to quit now. She worked quietly, traipsing up and down the ladder as she moved the string of lights around the tree, stretching her arms as high as she could without losing her balance.

The Simmonses' front door opened. "Let me hand you the lights," Erich offered, crossing the yard and coming up behind her.

Addie's initial reaction was to reject his offer. She was more than capable of finishing this—she'd managed the first tree on her own. She'd rather avoid Erich's company.

"It's the least I can do to make up for calling you Adeline," he said.

"If you had to place lights on trees for every time you called me Adeline, you'd be decorating the entire Olympic National Forest."

"True enough. It's Addie from now on. I promise."

She wasn't sure she should trust him not to be a jerk, but she was tired and hungry. So while it dented her pride to accept his help, at this point, she was willing. "Okay." The second part took more of an effort. "Thank you."

His sigh was audible. "That wasn't so hard, now, was it? Come on, Addie, admit it."

"Harder than you realize."

Erich chuckled.

He continued to feed her the string of lights, and they didn't speak for several seconds. "I talked to Jerry the other day. We stay in touch on Facebook, but . . ."

Addie finished and hurried down from the ladder. "Listen, Erich. You don't need to make small talk with me. We've never really gotten along and there's no need to pretend otherwise." She guessed he felt a little sorry for her—back at home, having failed at her big adventure. In her sad, decrepit car . . .

"Fine." He held up his hands as if she'd pointed a gun at him. "You can't say I didn't try."

"Thanks for the help with the lights," Addie said, before heading into the house.

———

Harry watched the scene, standing beneath an evergreen tree, from across the street. Celeste stood next to him.

"What is it I'm supposed to do for these two again?" he asked, unable to hide his dismay. It had seemed like a piece of delicious rum cake earlier, but now that he saw the way Addie bristled around Erich, he was a bit more daunted. She was like a porcupine around him, defensive and unfriendly. And that was only a small part of what he sensed in her. She was full of fear, and trying desperately hard to hide her feelings of inadequacy.

"You'll find out soon enough. God has obviously crossed their paths for a reason. There must be something they need to learn from each other, don't you think?" she said, turning the question back on him.

"Just how am I supposed to help them find out what it is when they can barely tolerate the sight of each other?" he asked. He was an English teacher and Addie was in his class. There was only so much he could do while teaching her literature.

"As I explained earlier, circumstances have been set in motion."

"Yes, but—"

"Patience, Harry, patience."

"Do you have an idea about what's going to happen?"

"I do."

Harry frowned. "Don't you think you should fill me in, seeing that I'm going to be working with Addie?"

Celeste grinned. "All in good time."

Harry wasn't pleased. "Is there anything else you want to tell me?"

"Not yet," she said, and tucked her arm around his elbow, shivered, and then glanced toward the sky. "Let's get back. The roads are getting icy."

Harry watched as Erich sped off in his shiny car. He had the distinct feeling Celeste had been trying to tell him something important.

ABOUT THE AUTHOR

DEBBIE MACOMBER, the author of *Dashing Through the Snow, Silver Linings, Last One Home, Mr. Miracle, Love Letters, Blossom Street Brides, Starry Night, Rose Harbor in Bloom, Starting Now, Angels at the Table,* and *The Inn at Rose Harbor,* is a leading voice in women's fiction. Nine of her novels have hit #1 on the *New York Times* bestseller list, with three debuting at #1 on the *New York Times, USA Today,* and *Publishers Weekly* lists. Her holiday novels, *Mr. Miracle, Mrs. Miracle,* and *Call Me Mrs. Miracle,* were all top-watched movies on the Hallmark Channel. In 2013, Hallmark Channel produced the original series *Debbie Macomber's Cedar Cove.* Debbie Macomber has more than 170 million copies of her books in print worldwide.

debbiemacomber.com
Facebook.com/debbiemacomberworld
@debbiemacomber
Pinterest.com/macomberbooks

Countdown to Christmas

Debbie Macomber's
Mrs. Miracle

Debbie Macomber's
Mr. Miracle

Debbie Macomber's
Call Me Mrs. Miracle

16 All New Premieres
Holiday Movies - All Day! All Night! | Starting November 1

AVAILABLE ON DVD
+ DIGITAL HD!

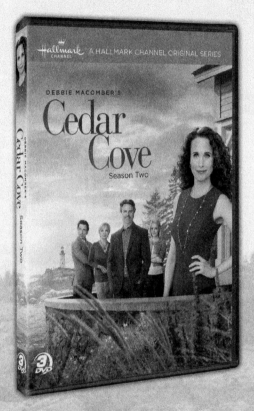

Based on the bestselling book series by the
#1 NEW YORK TIMES bestselling author
Debbie Macomber

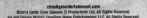

October 2015

Dear Friends,

My older cousins tell the story of sitting in a semicircle in front of my grandmother and watching her crochet. She was in her rocking chair, rocking away with her fingers moving at an incredible speed all while *she was sound asleep and snoring.* As best I can tell I'm the only member of our family who inherited this love of craft.

Knitting has played a large role in my life since the time I was a child. Because I'm dyslexic I struggled to learn to read. Learning to knit got me over the hump; reading the patterns helped with comprehension and reading skill, plus counting the stitches was practice in math. Little in life gives me more pleasure than creating knitting (or knitted) projects for those I love.

Something else that excites me is Christmas; it's my favorite time of year. My love of holidays is what has prompted me to write a holiday story for the last twenty plus years. And this year—drumroll, please—I'm including a knitting pattern along with this book. Something extra, something fun from me to you. (If you don't knit, then it's time to learn. You'll thank me later or curse me—depending on how successful you are.) If you're already a knitter, then enjoy.

Speaking of enjoyment, it's my sincere desire that you fall in love with Ashley and Dash and their madcap adventures as they struggle to reach Seattle for Christmas. I laughed my way through writing this book and hope this story gives you a reason to smile as well.

I always enjoy hearing from my readers. Your feedback has steered the course of my career. You can reach me through my website at debbiemacomber.com or on Facebook, Twitter, or Instagram (Are you impressed by how socially connected I am?) or by writing me at P.O. Box 1458, Port Orchard, WA 98366.

Merry Christmas.

Debbie Macomber

"Dashing Through the Snow" Hat

Finished size: Medium-Large Adult

Level: Easy

Yarn: Chunky weight #5

Needle size: 11 US (8.0 mm) 16" (40 mm) circular, 11 US (8.0 mm) Double Points

Gauge: 14 sts measured over 4" St st measured over unblocked swatch in the round

Abbreviations: CO-Cast On, sts-stitches, K-knit, P-purl, rep-repeat, Rnd-round, Rnds-rounds, beg-beginning, PM-place marker, M1-Make one, Inc-increase, K2tog-Knit 2 together, BO-Bind Off

CO 56 sts. Join being careful sts are not twisted. PM to mark beg of the Rnd.

Ribbing

Rnd 1-8 *K1, P1 rep from * to end of rnd.

Body

Rnd 1: knit

Rnd 2: (Inc Rnd) *K14, M1, rep from * to end of rnd. (60sts)

Rnd 3-4: knit

Rnd 5-6: purl

Rnd 7-10: knit

Rnd 11-12: purl

Rnd 13-16: knit

Rnd 17-18: purl

Rnd 19-22: knit

Crown Shaping
(change to double points when needed)

Rnd 1 *K13, K2tog rep from * to end of rnd (56 sts)

Rnd 2, 4, 6, 8, Knit

Rnd 3 *K12, K2tog rep from * to end of rnd. (52 sts)

Rnd 5 *K11, K2tog rep from * to end of rnd. (48 sts)

Rnd 7 *K10, K2tog rep from * to end of rnd. (44 sts)

Rnd 9 *K9 K2tog rep from * to end of rnd. (40 sts)

Rnd 10 *K8, K2tog rep from * to end of rnd. (36 sts)

Rnd 11 *K7, K2tog rep from * to end of rnd. (32 sts)

Rnd 12 *K6, K2tog rep from * to end of round (28 sts)

Rnd 13 *K2tog rep from * to end of rnd. (14 sts)

Rnd 14 Knit

Draw remaining 14 stitches up tight and fasten off securely. Weave in ends.

Make Pom Pom if desired.